UNM Unmapped territories.

$10.95 pb

Women In Translation

Publication of this book was made possible in part with support from the National Endowment for the Arts.

Cover design by Kris Morgan.

Library of Congress Cataloging-in-Publication Data
Unmapped territories : new womens's fiction from Japan / translated and edited by Yukiko Tanaka.
p. cm.
Translation of seven stories by contemporary Japanese women.
ISBN 1-879679-00-0 : $10.95
1. Short stories, Japanese--Women authors--Translations into English. 2. Japanese fiction--20th century--Translations into English. 3. Women--Japan--Fiction. I. Tanaka, Yukiko,
PL782.E8U5 1991
895.6′301089287′09045--dc20 91-24354
CIP

Printed in the United States of America
First printing, September, 1991

Contents

Introduction

Yukiko Tanaka

Unmapped Territories is the third anthology of Japanese women's fiction I have assembled and translated. The first book, *This Kind of Woman,* was a collection of stories written during the 1960s and 70s, an era of rapid economic growth in Japan. The second book, *To Live and To Write,* was a group of autobiographical stories written between 1913 and 1938—a politically liberal period when many women found it possible to write stories describing their struggles for autonomy. This third collection brings together some of the most recent works by Japanese women; all the stories were published during the 1980s, the "era of woman" in Japan.

The 1980s were years of transition in the lives of Japanese women—there were changes at home, in the workplace, and in society. Many of these changes were positive. Women were recognized as an important asset to the work force. The number of working women rose dramatically. In general, the presence of women in society was felt as it never had been before, in cultural, social and political arenas.

By the time the decade came to a close, however, it was clear there was a dark side to these changes. The divorce rate rose. Alcoholism among housewives became a public issue for the first time. Women with career ambitions who began emulating their traditionally hard-working male counterparts at the workplace discovered that they still shouldered the primary burdens of maintaining the home. The decade of the eighties was a turbulent time for Japanese women, filled with both the heady excitement and mounting stress of a society in flux.

There are some important similarities between the women represented in *Unmapped Territories* and those described in my second anthology, *To Live and To Write.* Both the 80s and the period from 1913–38 were periods of upheaval, when women worked to free themselves of traditional social and psychological constraints. In both collections we see women compelled by the pressure of history to explore unfamiliar terrain, to reinvent themselves.

The protagonist of "The Marsh," for instance, is a single mother raising two young children who rejects the traditional notions of "proper marriage" and motherhood. She continues to search for a relationship, but finds herself perpetually alone, outside the mainstream of society. She eventually shares her marginal existence with another rebellious single mother, a woman who shocks polite housewives at a PTA meeting by telling them how she graphically taught her son about the facts of life. "The Marsh" describes a growing solidarity between these women, who sometimes wonder if they are the "evil spirits of the mountains and rivers." The dark waters of the marsh evoke the internal landscape of a woman with her own myth buried deep inside.

The author of this story, Yūko Tsushima (b. 1947), has been introduced to Western readers through her previously translated books, *Child of Fortune* and *The Shooting Gallery.* She is a prolific writer who has won a number of important literary prizes. Tsushima is the daughter of the well-known writer

Osamu Dazai, who committed suicide with his lover shortly after the end of World War II. She has often used autobiographical material in her fiction, but in recent years she has integrated her experiences as a daughter and mother into more universal themes of women in historical transition.

In "A Family Party," Hikari Agata (b. 1943) describes a contemporary urban family dealing with the rapidly changing environment of Tokyo. The changes are seen through the eyes of a young mother, who witnesses the disintegration of her ancestral home and her old neighborhood. The story focuses on the tenacity of ordinary people who work to preserve traditional family life as land values rise and they are forced to relocate. The narrator and her relatives struggle to keep a feeling of rootlessness from engulfing their lives.

Agata went to work as a copywriter when she was in her early thirties. She wrote several stories based on her experience of raising two boys on her own after her divorce, one of which, "Humorous Explorers," received a 1982 New Writers' Prize. Agata's fiction is considered particularly noteworthy for its representation of the contemporary Japanese family as a changing social phenomenon. Besides writing about extended families, she has also pursued the theme of the eroding nuclear family, often describing the daily interactions between a single mother and her children. Agata has a refreshing sense of humor and an ultimately optimistic outlook on the possibilities of modern family life.

To the protagonist of "Sinking Ground" by Mizuko Masuda (b. 1948), Tokyo appears to have transformed itself beyond recognition. Noriko, a woman born in the far corner of this city, has seen it change dramatically—not only the urban landscape but the people, their values and relationships. Although she secures a small apartment room where she feels comfortably alone, various invaders threaten to break into her uneventful life—a rude neighbor who shows an awkward interest in her, an arrogant fellow worker whose self-confidence becomes increasingly oppressive. Despite Noriko's self-sufficiency and her contentment with being alone, these intrusions force her to venture into her past, into a landscape she has buried deep in her memory.

Noriko, an independent young working woman, is a character rarely found in earlier Japanese fiction. The popular terminology referring to a working woman like Noriko who is in her thirties and still unmarried, has changed over the decades from *oorudo misu* (old maid) to *hai misu* (high, or advanced maid) to, today, *shinguru* (single). The current term implies a lifestyle, like the one maintained by Noriko, free of family intervention and the meddling of others. Widely frowned upon only two decades ago, this lifestyle has become popular among young Japanese women, particularly in large cities. While Mizuko Masuda's stories are not necessarily autobiographical, the life of an independent woman is not unfamiliar to her: She left her parents' house when she was sixteen, put herself through college, and worked for the dentistry department of the Japan Medical School before beginning to publish her fiction. She received the New Writers' Prize in 1972. Masuda's stories often focus on independent women characters, exploring themes of separateness, what she calls the "single cells" of individuals. Like Agata and Tsushima, Masuda writes about women who are faced with new frontiers, women who want to advance yet are pulled backward by tradition and by personal memory.

An apartment in New York where a young woman can live by herself is the setting of the story by Eimi Yamada (b. 1959) entitled "When A Man Loves A Woman." Like many of Yamada's protagonists, the narrator here has an ambigious national identity; she could be Japanese or American. The only thing that's essential to the telling of the story is the fact that the main character is a woman engaged in a creative act. "When A Man Loves A Woman" is a love story told allegorically; Willy Roy brings the healing power of love from a warm climate in the middle of winter, allowing the protagonist to tap into her creative powers. The story is also ironic; while Willy Roy is presented as the quintessential gigolo, reinforcing the stereotype of African-American males held by the Japanese, he is a saviour nonetheless.

Among the writers represented in this anthology, Yamada is perhaps the freest with modern Japanese literary conventions. Frequently choosing African-Americans or other non-Japanese people as central characters in her stories and writing about them with sensitivity, Yamada seems to have fewer of the racial prejudices Japanese are often accused of harboring (though some of her fiction plays on the myth that black males are good in bed). Much of Yamada's work is sexually explicit, and her female characters, as in "When A Man Loves A Woman," hold a remarkably liberated view of sex; they are openly aggressive and take the initiative in sexual relationships. However, the focus in her fiction is not strictly on the erotic encounters themselves. Sexual conduct is seen as a direct expression of the values, world-views, and self-images of her characters.

Yamada, the youngest of the writers represented in this anthology, spent several years working as a cartoonist. Her use of English titles for her work ("When A Man Loves A Woman" is collected in a book entitled, *Soul Music Lovers Only;* other titles include *Bed-Time Eyes* and *Harlem World*) and her technique of using English expressions and profanity in her stories make them a bit strange at first for Japanese readers. However, the intrusion of incorrectly used English into Japanese conversation is a frequent occurrence, and no other Japanese writer has so extensively used this original and ironic stylistic approach. Yamada's fiction represents the tastes and preoccupations of today's young Japanese, who are sometimes referred to as *shin-jinrui,* or "new human race." As a recipient of the Naoki Literary Prize, given to works with excellence and broad appeal, Yamada has become one of the most sought-after writers of her generation.

In Minako Ohba's (b. 1930) story "Candle Fish," characters leave behind nationality to search for universal truths of women's experience. As in many of Ohba's stories, the protagonist of this story is a middle-aged woman who has left her native country, Japan. The women she encounters abroad are also exiles, at least in spirit. Olga, for instance, is a woman whose marriage to an egocentric musician has ended in bitter disappointment and estrangement from her true self. The narrator of "Candle Fish" forms a friendship with Olga as together they question their roles as wives and mothers. Many years after the two have ceased to see each other, Olga returns to the protagonist in her daydreams in the form of an ageless woman, the spirit of the moon. She both mocks and consoles the protagonist, who is transformed during these encounters into a *yamanba,* an imaginary folktale character who destroys men when they venture into her dwelling deep in the mountain.

The Japanese legend of the *yamanba,* or the old woman of the mountain, is used as the central motif in "Candle Fish" and in several other stories by Ohba. Although the *yamanba* commonly appears in legends as an old woman, Ohba sees her as ageless; she articulates repressed desires, and is the embodiment of all women who defy the constricting rules of society. Since her literary debut with the story "Three Crabs" (included in *This Kind of Woman*), which was awarded the prestigious Akutagawa Prize in 1969, Ohba has been exploring the tension contained in the figure of the *yamanba:* the dialectic between a woman's desire for independence and self-expression on the one hand, and the psychic pain resulting from her solitary existence on the other. Many of Ohba's stories are autobiographical, and Sitka, Alaska, where she lived for a while with her husband, provides the backdrop for "Candle Fish." Like the protagonist of this story, Ohba started writing seriously in her late thirties when she returned to Japan. She is a prolific writer still actively publishing, and is considered to be one of the most important Japanese women writers.

In contrast to Ohba, the approach of Kazuko Saegusa (b. 1929), who also writes fiction treating materials beyond her native culture, tends to be more bookish. Her literary debut came in 1969 when she received the Tamura Toshiko Literary Prize for women writers. After experiencing the trauma of the end of World War II while a student at a teacher-training school, Saegusa's first subjects had to do with the absurdity and uncertainty of human existence. It wasn't until the late 1970s and early 80s that she began actively exploring themes that could clearly be defined as feminist, publicly announcing at one point that she would only write fiction from a feminist perspective. Saegusa often writes about women who reject their traditional maternal roles, and has turned for source material to ancient mythology and Japanese literature. In more recent years she has written about the meaning of World War II from a woman's point of view.

"The Rain At Rokudō Crossroad," a short story Saegusa

published in 1987 in *Bungakukai,* one of Japan's major literary magazines, has a dreamlike quality. It is a ghost story, based on the legend of the ancient Japanese literary figure who travels back and forth between the world of the dead and the living. Saegusa eerily describes the transformation of an ordinary housewife into a strange and powerful woman. But the story is also based in the realities of contemporary Japanese life, where divorce is on the rise. The increasing independence of women is experienced by the male character in this story as a bad dream—an event outside his control. And the woman, too, experiences her freedom with a kind of dread and vertigo; while she's freeing herself of the past, she's also moving toward a future she can't predict.

Taeko Tomioka (b. 1935), represented here by her 1980 story "Straw Dogs," writes about female sexuality separated from its reproductive function and stripped of traditional moral codes. The story is a monologue from the point of view of a middle-aged woman who sets out on both serious and comic sexual adventures with younger men. Stepping aggressively into a traditional male role, she pursues sexual encounters one after another in an attempt to understand the true meaning of love-making. Neither romantic nor hedonistic, the "affairs" of this woman are more like voyages into truly unknown territory. The title hangs ambigiously over the story—straw dogs are used in Chinese religious rituals, and are burned to ashes when the ceremony is complete.

Born and raised in Osaka, with an early literary career as a poet, Tomioka has been a rebellious artist from the very beginning. She established herself as a fiction writer with the story "Family In Hell" (in *This Kind of Woman*), in which she scorned the traditional patriarchal family system as well as the trendiness of Tokyo. Many of Tomioka's stories explore the moral dilemmas of liberated women of the 1980s.

As in my two previous anthologies, I have tried to represent in this volume some of the best work by women writers, but I also hope to show new thematic and stylistic trends taking shape in contemporary fiction. Selecting stories for an anthology is always a difficult process. The decision of what to include was finally based on the enthusiasm I felt for the individual story. Another issue I had to consider was "translatability." Pieces that are written with great care in one language always present challenges in translating them into another. A style that works well in Japanese may prove problematic in English. One of numerous difficulties translators of Japanese fiction encounter is the issue of tense. Japanese tend to perceive time as a non-linear flow, and movement back and forth between different times is easily accomodated in the structure of their language. This is not the case with English. Since storytelling is inseparably tied to the concept of time, those stories which deal with memory, with the fusion of present and past, such as "Candle Fish," present the problem of trying to keep a story clear while doing justice to its complex time scheme. Readability is another issue. Since it is as important as accuracy I chose to eliminate small portions of "Sinking Ground" and "A Family Party." I have done this in such a way that the elimination does not harm the story as a whole.

After I finished translating all the stories, I discovered that there were some common themes. Dreams thread through the stories by Ohba and Saegusa, but the state of dreaming, of wandering through an unmapped region, is also a central experience of the protagonists of the other stories. This can be seen as a reflection of Japanese women's increased freedom to envision new experiences. It is also a sign of these women writers' willingness to be innovative in their literary techniques, to dream outside the old forms. Basing fiction on personal experience has been a strong convention in modern Japanese fiction writing, particularly women's writing. While some authors here use this approach, younger women like Yamada, Agata, and Masuda have made a clear departure from this tradition and write on diverse and socially relevant topics.

All the stories in this collection celebrate the flourishing imaginative lives of women. Delving into a territory unknown to herself, the protagonist of each story in the end begins to map her once-stifled inner life. And in this discovery of a rich interior world she shares, more than ever, the experience of characters created by contemporary women writers in other parts of the world.

UNMAPPED
TERRITORIES

The Rain at Rokudō Crossroad

Kazuko Saegusa

In the surrounding darkness the rain was black. He couldn't even see the tips of his fingers, yet there was a peculiar light around his feet. Perhaps it was because of the rain splashing back as it hit the ground. Even darkness like this must contain some light beams, he thought; water must reflect those beams.

Awhile ago there was a certain odor in the rainwater—a close, musty smell of wet soil. The smell of grasses and bushes being washed away.

The man didn't remember just when the rain had started, but he was sure it was after darkness had set in. Shortly after nightfall the red, near-full moon had risen, but soon it had disappeared without casting its bluish white light higher in the sky. Then deep blue clouds had spread over, covering both the western and the eastern parts of the mountain. Lightning flashed, zigzagging down from the clouds. The lightning was faint, and the thunder sounded far away. It won't rain anymore, the man had thought. Then suddenly it had started pouring. The rain closed in on all the streets of Kyoto; its force shook them.

"Will you let me in?" When the man heard the woman's voice, she was already under his umbrella. He stopped walking. Although he couldn't see her face very well in the darkness, she seemed to be young. He nodded.

"Which way are you going?" the man asked.

The woman didn't reply and continued walking. The man kept up with her pace. He wondered how far she wanted him to take her, thinking she might be a nuisance. But he wasn't annoyed—perhaps he could invite her to a nearby bar while waiting for the rain to stop. This thought cheered him up a bit.

A faint smell of the woman's hair floated inside the umbrella, and in spite of his age he felt excited. As if she knew the pace he usually walked, the woman walked along neither too fast nor too slow. Even his wife of nearly twenty years couldn't walk like this. His wife always complained that he walked too fast, that she always had to hurry not to fall behind.

The man turned a corner and headed in the opposite direction of his house. He didn't know if there were any bars in that direction, but stopping at a bar in his own neighborhood wouldn't be a good idea.

"Now wait a minute," said the woman. "Isn't this the wrong way?"

He was startled. This might be someone who knew him, one of his neighbors perhaps.

"I thought we'd have a drink or two somewhere. It'll stop raining soon." He stammered the words out. The woman sneered.

"If you don't want to, I won't insist. I'll take you back to your house." As he said this, he suddenly felt angry with himself. What had he done to deserve this strange woman? He should pull his umbrella back and just tell her to leave.

"I have no place to go," the woman said. She sounded contemptuous, as if sneering wasn't quite enough. "I don't have a house to go back to. But tell me, are you offended?"

"Did you leave your home?" the man asked, realizing that

he'd picked up someone he shouldn't have. He flinched.

"Leave home?" the woman said, beginning to laugh. As she laughed loudly she moved away, placing herself almost outside the umbrella.

"Don't be silly. How is that possible? I said I don't have a house."

"But, you. . . ." The man didn't know what else to say.

"Why don't we go to a hotel rather than a bar?" she said. Taken aback at her words, he assured himself that his hunch was correct; there's a technique like this in their trade.

"No thanks," he said, flustered. He tried to sound as uninterested as possible. "I don't buy prostitutes."

"Prostitutes?" the woman shrieked. "Why should I be a prostitute? I simply suggested that we go to a hotel."

When the man didn't say anything, she added, "I feel lonely. I don't like to be walking in the rain alone." Then she burst into tears.

He felt embarrassed. Luckily no one was around, but he still didn't want a young woman crying under his umbrella.

"But asking a stranger to go to a hotel is crazy. You say you are lonely, but we are all lonely, you see. . . ."

The man felt he had to say something to console her, to soothe her.

"Going to a hotel because you're lonely, that's a bit. . . ." When he repeated himself, she suddenly turned and looked at him.

"What's wrong with it? Are you a stuffy intellectual?" When he didn't respond, she went on, "Don't preach to me like a schoolteacher, please." Then she pressed her face against his chest and started sobbing.

It seemed to him that the woman's technique was rather

commonplace, but he thought he shouldn't be cruel. He put his hand on her shoulder and stroked it gently. As he kept stroking, he started to realize that he wouldn't mind going to a hotel with her.

It was still raining. There was no one around. At the end of the empty street that stretched in front of him there was a light, perhaps a street light, shining dimly. If he went to it, he knew he would be able to see better. But it seemed quite far away.

He stood still, holding the woman's shoulder in one hand and his umbrella in the other, until the woman finally spoke. The man couldn't hear her, so he held her face up to his.

"Kiss me." She said this in a very low voice. "We don't have to go to a hotel, so kiss me."

The umbrella was in his way, and he thought of letting it drop out of his hand. He wasn't a young man anymore, he reminded himself. Instead he put his arm around her hip.

She touched his lips with hers, lightly at first; then she thrust her tongue into his mouth.

"Let's go," the man said, as if he had made an important decision. His voice was surprisingly loud.

"Are you sure?" said the woman hoarsely. She looked up into his face, still leaning against him.

"I'm sure," he nodded, as if trying to reassure himself. "Now I'm feeling lonely too."

The woman sneered the way she had before.

"I bet you don't know where the hotels are," she said.

"No, I don't."

"You'd prefer not to go to one near your house, right?"

"Of course," the man smiled wryly. "But I don't think there are any hotels around here."

"I'm not from this neighborhood." The man made no reply, and the woman continued. "You haven't asked where my house is."

"Now that we've decided to go to a hotel, I don't want to know."

"You're right. For us this is what they call 'one-chance, one-meeting?'"

"That's an old expression."

"I don't really know what it means, but it seems to fit an occasion like this."

"I wonder who taught you that expression," the man said, pulling the woman toward him. By the movement of her shoulder he could tell she was laughing. Feeling ten, even twenty years younger, he walked with light steps. The rain had stopped. Now he was able to see the faintly lit street ahead of him.

The man wondered where he was—perhaps he was lost. But he couldn't be; he'd lived in this section of Kyoto for many years. Had he started walking in the wrong direction when he'd left the hotel? Still, why was the street this dark? He couldn't see a single street light in front of him now.

It was also strange that he could walk along even though it was pitch dark. He had lost his way and yet he went on walking. The street ahead of him appeared to be a dead end but he went on. It was like reading a story with an endlessly postponed conclusion. There were willow trees on both sides of the street. As he tried to recall which streets were lined with willows, he suddenly found himself on a much broader street. This must be either Oike Street or Horikawa Street, he thought. However, it wasn't clear whether the street ran south and north or east and west.

He walked along the broad street for a while, and once

again he came to a place where his field of vision narrowed. He could tell this although it was quite dark. Perhaps now he was on a narrow street. The space surrounding him seemed to be pressing against him from each side. He thought he had been walking straight, but in fact he had turned many corners blindly and had gotten lost. Just when he felt a strange sense of fatigue overtaking him he saw a light ahead, like the yellow light of a paper lantern.

"We've come to Rokudō Crossroad, haven't we?" a soft voice suddenly said by his ear.

She was right next to him, but her voice seemed to have come from a distant place.

"Rokudō?" At the moment he uttered this word, the man felt a heavy weight in his legs.

"If this is Rokudō Crossroad, we're at a dead end," he managed to say. The woman was silent.

"It's a dead end. I can't see an inch ahead," the man repeated as he peered into the darkness. The umbrella in his hand tipped over, letting rain fall on the woman's shoulder.

"I don't think it's a dead end," she murmured, heaving a sigh. "I'm sure we can go on walking."

"But I can't see the way."

"The way?" asked the woman, looking straight into his face and shaking her head. "There isn't any way. That's why we can go on walking forever."

The man felt uneasy. Ever since they'd left the hotel, he had been thinking there was something odd about her.

He had tried to leave her in the hotel, but when she saw him preparing to go, she'd put her clothes on in a hurry, like a pouting child.

"I'm coming with you," she had said, rushing out of the room before him.

"Oh no you aren't. I don't want you to come with me," the man had said. It was you who said 'one-chance, one-meeting,' he had wanted to tell her. Instead he had told her once again he didn't want her to leave with him.

"Don't worry, your wife can't see me," the woman said now, laughing as she walked alongside him. At that moment the man realized something was definitely wrong.

He shook his head. It can't be, he thought. It wasn't possible.

"What's the matter now? Why are you stopping?"

The woman had moved out from under his umbrella, but, in spite of the downpour, she wasn't wet at all.

"It's not raining on this side, you see," she said enticingly, letting her long hair stream in the wind.

The man couldn't think of anything to say; he felt a chill running through his body. No one his age who lived in Kyoto was ignorant of Rokudō Crossroad. The man recalled reading a description in a book: "Rokudō is on the south of Kennin Temple and it is a place from which Lord Ono Takamure used to depart for his journeys to Hades; hence it is often called the Way to Hades."

It was just an ordinary place during the day. When he had passed by it ten or so years ago, he was struck by its ordinariness. The temple called Rokudō Chinkōji didn't look as if it had a remarkable history. In the days when this was the road to the Toribeno burial ground, there might have been a forbidding atmosphere but now, with so many new houses being built. . . . He remembered feeling a bit disappointed at the time.

Flustered, the man tried to remember the route he'd taken since he first encountered the woman. He had been on his way home when it had started raining. His house was at Karasuma Kuramaguchi. Now he was altogether in the wrong place. Furthermore, the distance between his house and where he was now could not be covered on foot. He remembered making a U-turn away from his house, and since then everything had grown strange. The rain must have altered the appearance of the town. There was no other explanation. But no matter how long he walked, he had the sensation that an endless black concrete wall loomed up on both sides of the street.

"They aren't concrete walls. They are something the rain has made. Look, they're still here," said the woman from behind him, her hand on his shoulder. It was a heavy, cold hand, like ice.

He summoned his courage and grabbed the woman's hand. Her fingers were wet and so was the back of her hand. Then he touched her hair; it was wet, too. What he'd seen earlier, her dry, streaming hair, must have been an illusion.

"What's the matter?" asked the woman, pulling her hand away from him, smiling. "You thought I was a ghost, didn't you? If I were a ghost, I wouldn't have legs, but look here, I've got my legs."

What is it? he wondered; something is wrong. The woman's speech had changed subtly, now her tone was more familiar. Perhaps because he'd slept with her, but that was not all. As they approached Rokudō Crossroad, she suddenly looked older.

"These are damp," said the woman, trying to light one of his cigarettes. It wouldn't light no matter how many times she tried. The man shuddered, remembering a scene exactly like this.

"Why don't you take mine?" As he spoke, he shivered. He realized he'd said these exact words at another time.

"Thank you. You're kind." The woman smiled. Again, these were the same words. He had to struggle to keep his teeth from chattering. If this woman's face also became that of his lover's. . . .

"You look pale," the woman said, bringing the lighter close to his face after she'd used it to light her cigarette. "You're really pale. I wonder if you have a fever."

"I'm fine," said the man, heaving a deep sigh. The woman's face wasn't hers after all. It was a face with single-edged heavy eyelids over slightly slanted eyes, the same one he had seen earlier in the hotel bed.

There was something swaying at the bottom of this darkness and rain, something he had pushed away in his mind. He rarely thought about it now—not that he'd tried to forget, it was simply something that belonged to his past.

"I had a lover once," he said as if spitting out something that had been stuck in his throat.

"You have one now, too," the woman said disinterestedly, puffing her cigarette.

"No. I've got only my wife now."

"Your wife made you leave her?"

"No. This was before I was married."

"No problem in that case, is there?"

"She was much older than I was."

"I see."

The woman's face returned to the earlier disinterested

look, and she asked for another cigarette. Still, the way the woman smoked was just like his lover had. Instead of stretching two fingers straight and up, she had used her thumb and index finger to hold the cigarette, making a small circle, the way Jean Gabin did. The style might suit men of a stout build, but when women used it they looked like high school students smoking behind the teacher's back.

He'd gotten into the affair capriciously, but she'd told him she'd kill him if he left her; she'd kill him first and then herself. He didn't take her threats seriously. She didn't try to kill him, but she tried to kill herself with sleeping pills. She'd been in the hospital for about a month afterward. She was treated for a nervous breakdown. When she was discharged, she got married.

"I'll be the second wife of a man twenty years older than me, you see, and what went on between you and me was a dream," she had said, giving him a wry smile. At that time he'd had an urge to hold her in his arms but decided against it; he knew that if he didn't control himself, he'd be back in the same mess.

"What's the matter? You've gotten awfully quiet," said the woman. He pulled her cold hand toward him. He wanted the two of them to remain as they were for a while. The yellow lantern light was still swaying in the distance. It was strange that even though they had walked for a long time, they hadn't gotten any closer to the light.

It was not clear how much time had passed. The rain had stopped once again, and the nearly full moon was in the middle of the sky, casting its pale, silver-grey light on the landscape. The man and the woman were sitting on a riverbank, exhausted from walking.

When the man roused himself, he saw the woman sleeping with her head on his shoulder. He was about to put his jacket over her when she woke up.

"Oh, my. . ." She smiled, looking embarrassed. "I must have fallen asleep after crying."

"You didn't cry."

"Don't try to cheer me up," she said, twisting her face as if she were in pain. "Suppose you go home now. Yes, you go home and open the door. You find the rooms empty. There's a telephone sitting all by itself. What would you do then?"

The man did not immediately respond. He didn't know what she was trying to say.

"It's not possible that there would be only a telephone sitting there."

"Why not?"

"Burglars wouldn't do such a thing."

"Not a burglar," said the woman, and then she burst into tears. "I'm not talking about burglars. I'm asking what you would do if your wife was gone."

The man couldn't imagine his wife leaving. He became perturbed. He had assumed that his wife would always be there when he came home.

"You can't assume she will be there, you know. I've just left, today."

"You're married then?"

"I said I left, didn't I? I haven't signed the papers yet but I've left him. It's the first step anyway."

"Did you have a fight? It's easy to lose your temper sometimes."

"It wasn't like that. It was my conclusion after a long period of thinking."

"A long period? But you're not that old."

"If you've gone through it for a whole year, it's long enough," she snapped.

"He used to say I should leave when he wasn't around. So I did. He's gone on a three-day business trip, returning tonight. When he gets home, he won't find a thing, nothing but a phone. I called a used furniture dealer and sold all our furniture. I've got quite a lot of money from the sale. If we want to, we can afford to go to the hotel again."

This is extreme, the man thought, but he couldn't think of what to say.

"Your husband will be shocked. It's true you had a fight, but he wouldn't imagine anything like this. When he gets home and finds nothing there, that will be a bit . . ."

"You seem to know a stranger's mind rather well."

"Not a stranger. It's about me!" the man cried out. The words came out unexpectedly, and at that moment he felt the ground beneath his feet shake.

No, he hadn't thought about his own situation until now. He saw the sickly face of his wife in his mind's eye. Her paleness had become more unappealing after marriage; she had stopped wearing makeup. "I shouldn't have married," she'd said repeatedly, often right to his face. She'd had a good job at the city kindergarten but when the child was born she quit. Other women she worked with carried on, since the position of a city employee was a desirable one. But there was no one she could fall back on for help. It became too much for her to keep her job. "Not only do I look after the baby but another person as well," she used to say, referring to him.

Now their daughter was in junior high school. "Do you want to come with me when I get a job?" he'd heard his wife ask their daughter. "You can stay with your father if that's what you want." His daughter shook her head and said, "No, I don't want to because if I do, he'll make me cook every day." The two had laughed loudly.

She must be joking. It must be a joke.

He imagined a phone sitting in the middle of an empty room. Ten years ago he and his wife sold their old house in Anekōji Nishi Tōin and moved to a new condominium. When he arrived at their new home before the furniture had been delivered, he saw a black phone sitting in a space where no life could be felt, and it had unnerved him. An hour later his wife arrived with their daughter and all of their household belongings. Until then, he remembered, the room had looked like a prison cell.

"Are you going back to your house, thinking that your house is well-lit, that your wife awaits you with a late-night snack?" asked the woman reproachfully.

The man hesitated a little but braced himself to respond.

"I have no other place to go."

"You can stay here, then."

Here? Do you mean at this Rokudō Crossroad? the man wanted to ask, but he was afraid to utter the name. He remained silent. Having walked haphazardly in an unfamiliar part of the town, he'd lost his sense of direction.

"This must be the River Kamo," he said.

"It might be the Katsura River," said the woman.

"I was born here in Kyoto. I can tell the Kamo from the Katsura."

"You can tell?" the woman said with contempt in her voice and shot a suspicious glance at him. "What good does it do if you can tell?"

At that moment the man sensed that there was no way for him to ecape Rokudō Crossroad.

When it becomes morning, he thought, this enticement from Hades will vanish like a spell. He simply had to wait until then. This strange woman, who had been crying and laughing beside him, would also disappear, he reassured himself. And he'd be able to go back to his house where his wife and daughter waited. He wished the time would pass quickly.

"What's the matter? Can't you walk anymore?"

"I'm exhausted."

"The morning will be here soon," she said as if reading his mind. "But unless you walk, morning won't come."

"To tell the truth," she added when he didn't answer, "I want the morning to get here soon, too. But I don't think I'll make it. It's hopeless." There was a hint of tears in her voice.

Without waiting for him to respond she said, "You can make it—you can go back to your house."

The man and the woman sat there, staring at the flow of the river. Judging from the intensified clarity of the moonlight, he thought it must be past midnight. Rays of moonlight fell on the surface of the river and drifted about.

Neon lights on the other side of the river were still glowing. Are they on until morning? the man wondered. The lights seemed to be close enough to grab with his hands. If he wanted, he could go over there; he could even go now. He could cross the river. There was no bridge, however; somehow it had disappeared. He would have to walk in the water. It's not deep, he decided for no particular reason.

If I can go back and forth between this side and that side I'll be like Lord Ono, he said to himself. Actually, one doesn't have to be Lord Ono, anyone can do it any time—people simply aren't aware that they can.

The man looked again at the lights on the other side of the river. The colors were beginning to pale against the brightening sky.

Is this still Rokudō Crossroad? he wondered, turning around to look at the woman. She wasn't gone.

"You'll make it; you can go back to your house." He heard her voice, echoing from the bottom of his torn-out consciousness. He took a deep breath, as if trying to exhale the fatigue from his body. He heard the sound of a train in the distance. As he sat there, he thought it must be the first train of the day, running along the river.

Candle Fish

Minako Ohba

There is a woman who comes to me on sleepless nights, when I lie awake in bed imagining things.

I call her Tsukiko, the daughter of the moon, since she wears a robe that changes colors like the moon. Sometimes her robe is pale red, or the blurring color of milk; other times it is the sharp color of lemon.

She arrives on the back of the candle fish that come surging up on the shore of a moonlit cove; she flaps her sleeves, which might be the color of rose of Sharon blooming in the rain, or fading evening glories, or the silver-grey of pussy willows in early spring.

Candle fish are the small fish which appear suddenly on moonlit nights, covering the ocean shore with tiny popping sounds, and causing the water to ripple in all directions. Like Tsukiko, they shine and change colors in the moonlight. When you dry these fish and light them, they burn like candles.

Sometimes when I can't sleep I am transformed into a yamanba, the old witch of the mountain. It is then that Tsukiko comes to me. The yamanba runs through the mountains, letting her silver-grey hair flow in the breeze like flowers of pampas grass. She crosses the mountains effortlessly, from one ridge to another, as if she's flying, and in front of her is a man running as fast as he can, trying to escape from her.

This man is always a young man. He takes his clothes off as he runs and throws them one by one toward her, for he knows that the yamanba will pick up and devour anything that's in her path, giving him the chance to run further ahead.

The young man has stripped off most of his clothing and now has only his waist girdle[1] against his naked skin. He clutches his waist girdle tightly as he runs.

Regardless of what is beneath the waist girdle, this naked young man looks quite loveable to the yamanba. But it is what is inside that is precisely what she must eat. It is this that sustains her life, and it is because of this need that she has been chased away from the world of humans to live deep in the mountain.

Finally, the yamanba catches up with the young man. First she pulls away his waist girdle (which resembles the ones Japanese tourists wear abroad, opening them in dark corners of stores or in bathrooms, taking out a bundle of money to shop for a few brand-name items). But what she finds in the young man's waist girdle when she tears it away from him is something difficult to describe—it resembles the candle fish that have washed up on the moonlit shore, limp and shriveled.

When she tears it to pieces and begins to eat, she finds it to be tasteless. It looks a bit like a dead clam lying on the beach at night, but it tastes more like moist balls of dust.

After devouring it in one gulp, the yamanba feels sad. It hasn't given her the satisfaction she gets from tasting other foods, nor has it given her a sense of fulfillment. She sits on a cliff and starts to devour the lifeless body of the man. It is also tasteless. Blood streams down both sides of her mouth, and the

[1] *Pieces of cloth called "domaki," traditionally worn by men wrapped tightly around their lower torso.*

sound of the bones cracking away, like the sound of a cat eating a mouse, echoes through the valley.

When the sound of cracking bones reaches the valley, Tsukiko comes without fail. And like a candle fish glistening in the waves of the ocean, she undulates her hips and talks to me in a fish language, which resembles the sound of rippling water.

Looking down at me (this yamanba eating a man's body on the edge of a cliff), Tsukiko's face is like a candle fish—one who swam through the ocean of sky, across the mountain ridges, to stop and smile at me.

Tsukiko is a phantom who comes to me at night, but she was once a human female. She and I used to live by a narrow inlet at the northernmost corner of the earth, where one is reminded of the Ice Age. This inlet looked more like a river than a sea, and a cliff stood on its far side, covered by a dark coniferous forest that seemed suitable for yamanbas. We lived there, Tsukiko and I, at a spot where the inlet curved and a wet field of grasses stretched away from it. Situated on these lowlands by the sea, the place where we lived seemed like a mossy wasteland.

Once in a while I wonder how Tsukiko is doing now. The last time I saw her was some twenty years ago. We haven't written each other since then. Both of us know that we can't say what we really want to in a letter. But she visits me during the early hours of my many sleepless nights, when I turn into a yamanba.

At those times we sit face to face and talk in the language of candle fish. It's exactly what we used to do in days long ago when, on some nights when I couldn't sleep, I went to her house. Sometimes she would come to my house unexpectedly, and we would chat about this and that for a while.

I call the language in which Tsukiko and I talk candle fish language because when we talk neither the names we were given at our birth, nor our nationalities, nor the language we grew up speaking matters. We talk in a language that can only be understood between those who have lost the names given them at birth, the nationalities they were born to, and the language they have been raised to speak. Candle fish can swim to any shore of any country.

Perhaps you think I'm making up a strange story. I will now confess that Tsukiko has a real name, a Russian name, Olga.

I've read Chekhov a great deal since I was a teenager. Olga is the name of one of the three sisters in a play of his which I like very much. And when I used to look beyond the white clapboard house with the triangular roof where Olga, now Tsukiko, lived, I could see the mountain with the three peaks, which is called the Three Sisters.

Although she had a Russian name— perhaps after someone in her family—Olga was an American, born and raised in the United States. And I, of course, am Japanese. However, in these twenty years that Tsukiko has been visiting me during my sleepless nights, she has stopped talking to me in English.

I had lived for a long time in a small town where only a dozen or so Japanese people lived and people around me spoke English, so even after I came back to Japan, for some time my dreams were populated by people speaking English. Now I don't hear English in my dreams, but when I hear people talk, I'm not sure if it's Japanese, either. To me it sounds more like the language of candle fish. And I'd rather call her Tsukiko than Olga.

Perhaps because we lived by the inlet at the northernmost point of the earth, where we could see the midnight sun, Tsukiko now comes to visit me near dawn, in the half-light.

It was one of those summer nights when the midnight sun cast a pale light outside. In that pale light I was dreaming of becoming a yamanba. I felt like abandoning everything in my life, and I was in a state of anxiety that could only be calmed by running wild in the mountain and devouring everyone in my sight. Why would I run after them? Those travelers who knocked at the door of my solitary abode in the mountain did not necessarily care about me. They never told me what they really thought, plaguing my life with their politeness. Yet they expected blessings from the yamanba. These people reminded me of the hypocrites I'd seen in my younger days down in the village, and they made me angry.

Such deception, I thought, looking at my husband next to me, and at our child. They were sleeping peacefully but I couldn't. How could they sleep like that when I, his wife and her mother, longed to disappear? Maybe I would sleep soundly, too, if either of them had such a wish.

Feeling miserable, I got out of bed. I stood by the window and saw a light emanating from Olga's house. Between our houses was a small stretch of damp, moss-covered land where some pine trees stood among the buttercups and the cowberries with their small white flowers. I could get to Olga's house if I walked twenty yards or so. I called Olga, even though it was almost midnight, and she answered.

"Why don't you come over," she said.

I hesitated, knowing that she had to get up early in the morning. I'd only wanted to chat with her on the phone. But she said she was going to take the next day off anyway.

"I've accumulated a week's vacation time. I've got to take it by the end of this year, and I've decided to go ahead and take a day off whenever I feel like it. I can't afford to take a trip, so I'm going to stay home tomorrrow and do nothing. I've just baked a loaf of pumpernickel bread. Why don't you come and eat it while it's still warm and have some coffee with brandy?"

When I glanced in the mirror, I looked like a ghost. But the ghost changed her clothes and left her house, trying not to make any noise.

A dog barked while I was crossing the desolate land; it sounded like a wolf. As I walked, the wet ground sank under my feet, soaking my socks. Walking on the moss-covered ground in summer was always like that. In winter, the frozen ground would resist the shoes walking over it and make a small, hard sound. I saw the Three Sisters looming up beyond the roof of Olga's house. The mountain was bare, with a few patches of snow here and there. How many years have I lived here looking at this view, I wondered as I walked.

I was still in my twenties, but I felt like the old cedar tree that had been standing at the foot of the Three Sisters for thousands of years. Dry moss hung from some of the branches of the cedar, looking like long white shrouds of hair; higher up on the tree I sometimes saw a bald eagle perched in perfect composure. The eagles were near extinction in most places but some still survived in the northern regions where we lived.

I was born and raised in Japan, an ancient country with a long history, but when I lived there I had never felt like an old cedar. Yet when I separated from my country a strange part of me, which seemed to have been covered by moss before, revealed itself. I became aware of a power inside me, informing me of things I had no way of knowing.

I was at the age when one tends to be easily discouraged by

one's own selfishness, and I was feeling uneasy about my marriage. I had known I wasn't the type who would easily adjust to marriage. I had agreed to come to this remote foreign land because I wanted to see something new. But when I saw it, I began to yearn again for something else, still not knowing what I actually desired.

We are the creatures who dream about things we cannot attain. Our dreams do not exist in reality.

If I had told my husband that I wanted to go back to Japan, where my search had originated, he might have agreed to return. But that wouldn't have been the solution for me. I would have repeated the same pattern of wishful dreaming there, too.

Perhaps I would have dreamt of something else, but I would be dreaming nonetheless. I thought I might be better off if I disappeared like smoke. Since I seemed to be drifting anyway, I would have preferred to actually evaporate into the atmosphere, like steam coming in contact with cold air. Then I could become snow and fall on the peak of the Three Sisters. In summer I could sink into the earth under the hot sun.

Yet I knew that, even then, I would crawl out from under the ground and look into the sky; I would sit with my arms wrapped around my knees, and I would dream. And even if I could really disappear like vapor, leaving my husband and child to sleep soundly like the earth itself, I would fall again somewhere, sometime. It is not possible even for smoke to become nothing.

I am awake now as I was in those days, and I am thinking of the Three Sisters in that remote land. Someday I shall go back there to see the mountain, and I will murmur those famous lines to myself: "There's nothing I want to say to the mountain; so precious is this mountain of my native place."

The time I spent in the shadow of the Three Sisters was the most precious period in my life, a time when I searched for meaning beyond words. It was the time when I had no other choice but to try communicating with people in my broken English. If conversation in Japanese had been possible, I would have enjoyed it, at least the rhetorical aspect of it, but with my English such enjoyment was rare.

I am remembering a night twenty years ago. I visited Olga that night, having crossed the barren land in the pale dusk. A desolate, colorless wind was blowing. Up in the ghostly sky, I saw the Three Sisters huddling. A dog barked, sounding like a wolf in the distance.

When I arrived at Olga's house, the door opened as if she'd been standing there waiting for me. The smell of fresh pumpernickel bread streamed out.

"I made this with plenty of honey in it, just the way my grandmother taught me. When it rose, I kneaded it again and let it rise one more time so that it's nice and firm," said Olga, looking proud of herself.

What made her bake pumpernickel late at night when her children had long been asleep, I wondered. Is it only the sudden mood of a mother so busy she rarely has time to spare for her children?

Olga divorced her husband when her children were still small. She worked as a bookkeeper at a cannery.

She once told me that when she received her first paycheck and saw the amount written on it, she cried. It wasn't an amount she and her two children could live on. It was not much more than what her alcoholic husband now and then gave her before their divorce.

"How could you do it? Divorcing your husband with two children to look after?" I once asked her. I was impressed by her courage. Twenty years ago divorce was quite rare in Japan, and no one would hire a single mother with small children.

"You can do it if you want it badly enough," Olga told me.

She took a few more jobs bookkeeping for small shop owners in town and managed to make a living for herself and her children.

When she was young Olga had fallen in love with a musician. A stranger in a small town, he was selfish and proud—like many artists. Her parents were naturally unhappy about the situation and sent Olga away to college in the city, hoping she would forget about him. She was madly in love, though, and left school at the end of first term to be with him.

Olga believed in her husband's talent, which he revealed to her often, and she convinced herself that he was a genius.

"Then he started drinking," Olga told me. "He became abusive. But still I thought he was a genius, or at least I tried to keep thinking so. He had a talent for bringing something special out of music, a kind of maddening beauty. But he lost interest in the small town orchestra he had been conducting, and started to verbally abuse the people in it—he didn't know what else to do.

"He was angry at not being invited to conduct a better orchestra, and so he found fault with the people around him. He imagined invisible enemies, and he drank in order to stimulate his imagination.

"Soon he stopped giving me money to run the house. One day, when I saw the half-torn lace of my threadbare underwear,

I felt so sad. 'How can you let your wife wear underwear like this?' I asked him. He threw a ten dollar bill at me." Olga's face twisted in pain when she told me this. Ten dollars at that time would be thirty or fifty now, I thought.

"I went shopping and walked the street, feeling like a beggar. I stopped at a display window where I saw a mannequin showing off some pretty underwear; I looked for a moment, and then I walked away. I went into the music store next door, and for a while I listened to the record the salesgirl played for me. When I left the store I had two Bach records in my hand. Instead of underwear I bought records. I wore my old underwear until I divorced my husband.

"By the way, after I bought the two Bach records, we were happy for a while," Olga added.

But it was not because of her miserable underwear that Olga had divorced her husband. He insulted her in a way that hurt her deeply. Perhaps he said something he shouldn't have, or maybe it was simply his openly disrespectful attitude.

Olga's husband felt his talent was wasting away, and naturally he blamed his wife and children. He became abusive toward his children and started to swear at them as if they were his crooked, annoying fingers. He became angry not only at them but also at Olga, who had agreed to have them.

One day he hit Olga, and the younger child attacked him with a broom. The father threw the child against the wall like a ball. Olga decided then to take her children and leave her husband.

"When we signed the divorce papers he looked relieved, as if his burden was finally lifted. But still, the expression on his face wasn't that of a man who knew he could get his confidence back if he freed himself of his wife and children. I felt sorry for him, and I nearly changed my mind. But then I remembered what he'd said to me, that he'd almost killed me with those words. So I left. If you try to kill someone, you can't complain about being killed yourself, can you? By putting his hand around my neck, he slowly strangled himself. That's what happened."

What were the words that would take the life out of a woman? I wondered at that time. I've been asking myself this question ever since.

"I imagine his music is also dead now," Olga said quietly but clearly, concluding her story. Her words sounded like a curse. "There's no doubt that a man who would kill a woman will be killed by her." Shortly after Olga left him, her husband was put in a hospital for alcohol treatment.

Olga didn't tell me the details of her divorce except the story about her underwear, which I knew wasn't the real issue. And yet I felt I understood. I accepted her divorce.

In those days the curly hair covering Olga's forehead was the color of a fire blazing in the sun, but her pubic hair was darker. When we went swimming, it looked like seaweed floating in water along a snowy beach. She and I often went swimming together in the city pool. She was taking lifesaving lessons. Perhaps she was trying to find an extra job as a lifeguard.

Olga, like many women in her country, didn't hesitate to show her nakedness to other women, but I felt overwhelmed by all of the naked bodies standing around me in the locker room. Those women would even have quite ordinary, cheerful conversations while they peed noisily.

When I was a young woman in Japan I lived in a dormitory for nearly ten years; I was used to seeing naked women. But I was still shocked by the atmosphere in the locker room. How different a mood women's nudity could create in different circumstances. It was at this time I realized that just as paintings of nudes in Western art had a long history of their own, Japanese paintings had a different perspective unique to themselves. It seems we discover the meaning of our unconscious behavior only when we are confronted with the unconscious behavior of others.

In any event, Olga and I used to stand under the locker room shower together, each thinking about things that were foreign to the other. We became friends through talking together, stopping here and there in the convoluted process of getting to know one another.

It also helped that my daughter was the same age as her son. They played together often, and sometimes I would absent-mindedly listen to their chatter. For instance, one day as I was lying near the window reading my book, I heard them sing a song while they played with sand:

Dark bread, white bread,
Spread the butter, spread the jam,
Put in some honey, stick in the cheese,
Wrap an olive with some bacon,
Add a pear, grapes, and almond trees.

I looked over and saw they were pretending to be bakers. They were kneading mud, forming it into various shapes, decorating these shapes with petals of buttercups and other flowers. When they finished, they put the mud cakes on a large banana tree leaf.

The children had made such feasts for Christmas parties, for Easter, and once for Halloween.

On that Halloween, Olga's son and my daughter were outside acting out their respective roles, saying something to a pine tree and a mountain ash. Judging from the way Olga's son cried and kicked his legs, I thought he must be pretending to be a baby; he crawled around and moved his lips like a baby sucking its mother's breast. Then he stretched his neck and moved like a ghost, and embraced the trunk of the pine tree.

Ghosts in Western stories usually look quite imposing; they challenge, even mock their opponents—not like Japanese ghosts, which are legless and mournful and wave their arms in a dejected manner. Halloween ghosts are usually cheerful and noisy.

Now Olga's son was howling like a baby as he grabbed onto the pine tree; my daughter meanwhile was holding a tree branch between her legs and pretending to be a witch, circling around the mountain ash.

"You're bad, making my mom unhappy," said Olga's son to the pine.

"Look nice, Mommy. You look bad when you twist your mouth, and we step on bad faces," shouted my daughter, confronting the mountain ash.

When I heard this, I remembered the time my daughter stuck her fingers in the corners of my mouth to make me look less glum. I realized then that I was a selfish mother who allowed her young child to see the mean face of a yamanba.

I also remembered the time when I was shocked by the pictures the two children had drawn. Olga's son drew the angry face of his father with a wide open mouth and hair standing up; and my daughter drew me with my mouth and eyes sadly sagging.

The children's Halloween play made me feel so uncomfortable that I wanted to look away. But I forced myself to keep watching.

The baby ghost and the witch on her broomstick were in

good spirits for a while as they circled round and round the pine and the mountain ash like two honey bees. As they grew tired, however, their play took on the air of a ritual, like a secret mass held in the basement of a church. Finally, they went back to their mud cakes, and ceremoniously carried them to the trees. They started feeding the trees by pressing the cakes onto the trees' imaginary mouths. They chanted:

Dark bread, white bread,
Spread the butter, spread the jam,
Put in some honey, stick in the cheese,
Wrap an olive with some bacon,
Add a pear, grapes, and almond trees.

On the moss-covered desolate land, over which the children's song traveled, the ragged pine trees and mountain ashes quietly cast their long shadows in the late afternoon sun.

After they finished their play, the children headed toward Olga's house, where a woman looked after them while Olga was at work. Since nothing stood between my house and Olga's except the scattered trees, I was able to see this woman moving about inside the house. According to Olga, she was an excellent, conscientious babysitter. I imagine she even managed to watch her charges from a distance when the children came to my house to play. She was an Armenian in her fifties. Whenever I saw her in town she smiled at me, displaying two big rabbit-like teeth. This smile made me feel slightly uneasy every time we saw each other. I couldn't help wondering what was hidden behind her steel-blue gaze.

Olga's babysitter must have watched the children's Halloween play from her window as I had from mine. Just as Olga's son came to my house to play, my daughter went to Olga's; she had juice and cookies there. The babysitter might have seen the same pictures the children had drawn of their father and mother; she might have been impressed by their vividness. I pictured her giving the children cookies to reward them for their excellent drawing.

Once a couple of fresh wreaths of flowers—which the children had evidently stolen from the cemetery—were placed by the pine tree and the mountain ash. Startled by the children's behavior, I immediately took them back to the cemetery. I let the children out of the car by the entry, and they lifted the chain and went inside.

"People who loved the dead person put these flowers on their grave, you see, and so they belong to the dead person. If you remove them, you're stealing. Do you understand?" As I said this to the children, I sensed the banality of my words. I was ashamed of myself. But another thought crossed my mind: the children might have placed those wreaths on the graves of their parents, whom they imagined they had killed. This thought frightened me and I uttered some commonplace words in order to distract myself.

I didn't tell Olga about my frightening thoughts. Whenever I sat with her, I would keep looking down, my mouth full of words that might describe what I had seen and what I had felt. However, when I saw Olga's curly hair shining red-gold in the sun, and the sweat on her forehead vaporizing into the air, I saw my words slip out of my lips, freed of their entrapment, rising into the air to entwine themselves in Olga's hair. On these occasions, I thought Olga's Armenian babysitter might appear from nowhere and flash her rabbit smile at me, showing her two big front teeth.

Sometimes Olga's son brought a sack lunch to my house. As in the song he and my daughter sang, his bag was filled with such things as honey on cheese, almonds and olives wrapped with bacon. Since my daughter looked envious, I had to fix something for her that would match his lunch. Seeing what Olga was able to do in the morning before she went to work, I tried my best to make a nice lunch for my daughter.

Olga's son had freckles on his nose and his eyes were the color of a clear autumn sky. "He's becoming more and more like his father," Olga told me once, "or maybe I should say his father must have looked just like him when he was a kid." Eating a slice of pumpernickel bread, she added, "He plays piano even though no one has taught him; he can play by ear."

In the days when she was in love with her husband, Olga had practiced her piano seven hours a day. It would have been easy, then, for her to teach her children how to play, but she seemed to resist it and instead tried to discourage them.

After a while Olga played occasionally when her children had gone to bed. Perhaps her son listened from his bed, or maybe he listened to records during the day when his mother wasn't around. At any rate, Olga's son had a good ear and played piano without being taught.

Olga's daughter was a hot-tempered child. She had a deep voice and a habit of running her hand through her long, straight, platinum-blond hair.

"Among the various things we inherit from our parents, emotion is more genetically determined than anything else." Olga once told me, reporting what she had read somewhere. She seemed disturbed by this finding.

"They say what the parent has the power to do is to foster will power," she added. She was worried that her children would eventually show some of their father's undesirable traits, and she was eager to find ways they could develop their will power and curb their unruly emotions. When she examined her children she saw her ex-husband, and when they felt their mother's cold, detached stare, they flinched. Yet they were helpless. Having no one else to turn to, they held on to their mother.

It's only a matter of time until Olga's children learn to stop depending on her, I thought. They would soon learn to justify and live with the strong temperament they had inherited from their father. When that time came, they would leave their mother behind.

When she left her husband, Olga decided that artists were not good for a happy family life. Whenever she met a person with an artistic temperament, she would pull an imaginary seal marked "scoundrel" out of her pocket and place it on that person. It seemed she had developed an unusually keen ability to spot individuals with artistic temperaments. When I was getting acquainted with her she tried to put this seal on me, and she would have done so if I hadn't been careful.

I had been intimidated by Olga in the days of our early friendship. Every time I met her I thought about telling her that I was a writer, but I hesitated. Since I hadn't published any work yet, I had no reason to tell her; yet keeping this from her made me feel uneasy. I knew I was a writer and nothing else, it was a fate I was powerless against. So, by not telling her, I felt I was lying about myself.

This was why I felt awkward in front of Olga, and, sensing this, she looked for opportunities to affix her seal to me. On such occasions she appeared to be enjoying herself.

Olga believed that all those who are drawn to art are scoundrels acting under the delusion that their shabby egos are essential to their artistic creations. She felt she had to identify these people in order to protect herself from their sweet charm, which they used to trap whoever came their way.

Despite such precautions, Olga tended to be hopelessly attracted to people with artistic tendencies. She seemed to spot them easily, and she considered it her special mission to put her seal on them. Like the secret police, who feel thwarted when they have no offenders to ferret out, Olga felt disappointed if there was no one around her with an artistic temperament. When she spotted such a person, she became deeply excited and approached them with shining eyes, looking like a moon goddess.

I had no reason to resist Olga's attempt to put her seal on me. I felt sorry for her and was afraid of disappointing her. A part of me wanted to prolong the game and let Olga enjoy it. Perhaps it was in this kind of game, I thought, that I could produce work as a writer. I looked forward to the time when I would finally complete my work and allow Olga to rightfully stick her seal on my forehead. Meanwhile I swam in front of her like a candle fish, trying not to be caught in her hand.

I once told her about the yamanbas who chase men through the mountains and devour their bodies after catching them. I pretended I was simply telling her an old Japanese legend.

"I'll never lose my way the second time. I won't knock on the door of a hut where a yamanba lives and be eaten alive," she said. Since I had told her it was "a person" rather than "a man" who ran from the yamanba, she imagined herself fleeing from the yamanba.

"I ran away from my husband, naked, and I took with me only one thing, the sense of myself, you see," she said.

For whatever reason, Olga stopped trying to close in on me and place her seal on me after I told her the story of the yamanba. She kept her distance from me and observed me with caution.

"I agree, yamanbas should live alone in the mountains," Olga said. "A few people who ran fast must have escaped and told the villagers about them, and that's how the story has spread. But in my opinion mountains would be totally uninteresting unless there were yamanbas," she added. When she chuckled, I was a bit frightened of her. "Let those people say whatever they like; it's best to stay away from them."

When Olga used the phrase "those people," it seemed she was referring to both the yamanba and the people she called "scoundrel." On those occasions she looked like a person dreaming about something unattainable. I thought she must have had the same expression on her face during the brief happy moments with her husband after she had bought two records instead of new underwear.

On that night, sipping coffee with brandy at Olga's house, the sound of music came down from the attic room. It wasn't Bach but a song that was popular among teenagers at the time.

"When I'm sixteen, on my birthday

I am going to run away. . . ."

"It's one o'clock. Go to sleep," shouted Olga, and the music stopped. The children might have wanted their mother to hear that music.

"What I wanted when I was young, and what I've actually done! These kids are finally getting to that stage. Even though there are lots of examples like me, people still make that kind of song, as if they don't know any better," she said and shrugged her shoulders.

"But we don't learn from other people, I guess. If I were ten years younger, I'm sure I would do the same thing all over again. That's why I don't want to be younger. Why do people want to bring their youth back? For my part, I'm glad it's gone for good." Olga, who was then only just past thirty, smiled.

That night was the last time we talked. She remarried and left town. Her new husband worked at a marine biology institute somewhere. Later I heard news about her from a mutual friend. Her daughter, I heard, ran away on the day she turned sixteen, and her son was with an orchestra somewhere, playing the drums. It was said he'd decided not to get married or have children. No one knew what had happened to either Olga's runaway daughter or to the father of her children.

Olga came to me by my bed this morning. She wore a moon-colored robe and sat on the window sill with a characteristically taunting smile on her face.

"Do you want to eat this? " she said as she took something out of the waist girdle she had tacked inside her robe. It looked like dried candle fish.

"Here, take it," she said and threw it at me as if she were offering it to a beggar.

She was no longer Olga but Tsukiko with her shiny skin reflecting the moonlight. The moon does not give light of its own; it simply reflects other light to become either young or old, a full moon or a thin new moon. Sometimes it disappears completely, making the night pitch dark.

The Olga I remembered, who had held onto her precious

self even when she was stripped naked, has gone somewhere forever.

"You are not putting your seals on people anymore?" I asked.

"I've lost all my seals," Tsukiko said in the voice of a candle fish. At that moment the candle fish flickered as if it were a flame, and the curly hair on her forehead shone—the color of the moon.

Sinking Ground

Mizuko Masuda

Any person living in an apartment alone would be disturbed by someone banging so hard on their thin door. Noriko had just returned from work and was changing, her clothes scattered on the floor. The room was small enough to take in at a single glance, and there was no place to hide. Noriko stood still, held her breath and tried to listen. She wasn't expecting anyone, and she hadn't done anything that might cause someone to come and complain. She didn't want to answer the knocking, which seemed unreasonably rough and loud.

"Hello, it's me, Sugio. Your neighbor. Are you home?" the visitor finally called out after banging for some time. Noriko, still in her underwear, couldn't immediately respond.

She hurriedly put on her clothes and opened the door slightly. The strong smell of machine oil floated in.

"What is it?"

"You got the evening paper?"

"What about the evening paper?"

"I want to see it now. You've got it, don't you," Sugio said. Before Noriko could reply, he spotted the paper lying near her feet, unopened. As he leaned over to pick it up, Noriko jumped aside a bit, and he spread out the paper right there, eagerly and unabashedly.

Awhile ago Sugio had asked Noriko if she'd mind sharing

her paper with him occasionally, declaring, "There's no need for all of us to subscribe to a newspaper. That'll only make some rich guys even richer. If there's important news, you'll hear about it anyway, and even if you don't, it wouldn't make any difference as far as your own life's concerned." He had just moved into her building and by then she'd already said hello to him a few times. Noriko didn't pay much attention to this explanation; it sounded like a line he probably used to meet women. But then he surprised her and said, "I'll give you movie tickets instead. I can get them at a discount price." She thanked him and smiled, unable to resist entertaining faint expectations. This conversation had taken place about a month ago, and since then Sugio had brought one ticket in exchange for a bundle of newspapers, which he never returned. The ticket had been good only on weekdays, and Noriko couldn't use it. From then on, she decided to be cautious about Sugio's charm.

Noriko sighed and looked down at Sugio, who was still trying to find the article he had supposedly come for. He was on his hands and knees like an animal, paying no attention to the fact that his dirty work pants were rubbing against the newspaper and her tatami floor.

Frankly, Noriko preferred not to have anyone touch her papers even after she had finished reading them. Reading her paper while listening to the television news was one her few pleasures. So Sugio's audacity was beyond her. Next, he might say that living alone in an apartment was wasteful, only helping the landlord make more money, and suggest that he move in with her.

"Please be careful with them. I hate having to read papers that have been handled a lot. What are you looking for anyway?" Noriko said slowly, trying to stay as calm as she could.

From her experience at work, she knew that even the slightest display of irritation or anger might cause her to be labeled a hysterical woman.

"I found it!" Sugio cried out, clutching the paper up high. He paid no attention to Noriko.

"It's right here. That accident was real after all," he said, more to himself than to Noriko. Then he thrust the paper toward her, keeping his finger on the article.

It was a small article printed in the lower corner of the page. A high school couple riding a motorcycle had crashed into a house and died, the article said. They had evidently tried to avoid a car coming in the opposite direction but failed.

"I saw the accident. When they hit that car, they flew up in the air at least three feet. They didn't look like human beings. Their arms and legs were all stretched out, as if they were swimming. It was like watching a silent movie. There was no sound. We were in our car, and my buddy, who was driving, didn't see it; he just went on driving as if nothing had happened. I didn't think of telling him to stop, either. We were passing them just as it happened, and I turned around and watched the whole thing. When we got back to our office, I started thinking that maybe there hadn't been any accident. Not a single car stopped; they just kept moving as if everything was fine. Pedestrians, too. It was as if nobody saw anything. Really, it's true."

Sugio stared at the article, which was only a few lines long, for a long time. Then he burst out again:

"The woman flew to the wall and stuck there, flat. It took several seconds for her to fall to the ground. I'd been watching the motorcycle before it happened, 'cause the girl was teasing the guy, putting her hand in front of him. She was pulling down the zipper of his pants in the middle of the road. Can you believe that? The guy got flustered and turned his head. He didn't see the car coming in his direction. They flew in the air, one holding on to the other. I think it served them right." While he talked, Sugio was fiddling with the zipper of his work pants. "The girl was lighter, I guess, so they came apart as they flew. She went as far as the wall, but the guy didn't. Come to think of it, I must have seen the whole thing really well."

Noriko turned her face away from Sugio and tried to envision a scene in which a boy and girl flew in the sky, embracing each other. What came to mind, however, was the girl stuck awkwardly to the wall. Was she facing the wall, or the other way? Was her head up or down? She imagined all of these possibilities, but none of them seemed real.

"What a weird experience that was. I felt strange all day. It was a big accident but they've made it into such a small article in this paper. I don't get it. But my buddy, sitting right next to me, didn't even know it happened. Well, you can't trust the newspapers, I'll say that," Sugio continued. Having taken his hand from his zipper, he now crossed his legs and looked at the paper intently.

"Can I have the paper?" Noriko said, getting hold of herself. She took it from Sugio and tore out the article as he watched in amazement.

"You can have this. That'll do, won't it?" she said. Sugio took the piece of paper thrust at him and held it between two fingers, looking puzzled. Then he stood up as if he'd suddenly remembered something.

Noriko did not read that evening's paper, and the accident was not reported on television. The news was focused on a plane crash that day. A domestic flight from Fukuoka to Haneda had missed its landing and crashed into the sea, where the water was only about a meter deep. Noriko had heard about a similar accident just days before—a U.S. airplane had failed to take off and crashed into a frozen river. Only four or five people survived this accident but the one near Haneda took twenty-four lives, leaving about one hundred and fifty injured.

People who fly in the sky fall down while those who run on the ground fly, and both cases excite the rest of us who do neither, thought Noriko. She had never flown in an airplane or ridden a motorcycle. She couldn't imagine how it would feel to fly or to fall. Even though he had scrutinized the paper Sugio hadn't even noticed the article about the plane crash, which must have had a big headline. Noriko found him to be even more peculiar.

I don't fly on airplanes, Noriko told herself, lifting the curtain and looking up at the dark, starless sky outside. It seemed not altogether impossible that a plane could fall through the low hanging cloud in front of her eyes, or a person on a motorcycle could crash through her window. Straining her ears, she heard her heart beating louder and louder. There had never been an occasion, however, when Noriko had heard the sound of an airplane engine in her room, and the streets surrounding her apartment building were too narrow and winding for a motorcycle to run at full speed.

But life-and-death incidents, the kind that are reported in newspapers, had occurred to people close to Noriko more than a few times. Each time she hadn't learned of them until later, when someone had told her. They had taken place and they were done with before she was made aware of them.

When she was in the tenth grade, one of her classmates committed suicide on the school playground by setting himself on fire. This happened in the middle of the night, and by the time the students came to school someone had sprinkled sand on the ground where the burning had taken place. They dug a hole and took some sand from the sand box, and no one went near there until new sand was brought in. The student who died was a quiet type, and no one knew he had been suffering.

The girl who died by crashing against the wall was sixteen, the newspaper article said. The same age as the classmate who had burned himself to death, Noriko realized. The girl had cut her classes to take a motorcycle ride with the boy; she had teased him with his pants zipper. She must have done all sorts of things Noriko had never tried and couldn't imagine. And now she's no longer in this world. Did her parents know what she was thinking? How many of her friends were aware of what she was doing?

Noriko pulled the newspaper toward her and touched the area around where the article had been torn. Violent deaths and insensitive witnesses. She stared at the rough-edged hole in the paper, and felt a surge of distrust toward people in general. She didn't think of herself as a misanthrope, though she was aware that people at work talked behind her back, calling her sullen and mean. But she couldn't understand why Sugio, for instance, who was so eager to find the article, didn't think of stopping at a newsstand and buying his own paper. She thought of Tsukamoto, a new employee she worked with, and his sociable but often insolent attitude. She wondered why he and Sugio seemed to be more lively than she was. It was somehow unfair.

Tsukamoto worked hard, no doubt; he was a cheerful young man with a bright future.

The established tea serving custom at Noriko's workplace was self-service, with the exception of the top executives. New employees had been informed of this, and yet when a female staff member stood up with her tea cup, Tsukamoto would say, with a friendly smile and without a moment's hesitation, "Can you make some for me, too?" This had been repeated so many times that young female employees made a point of serving him whenever they made tea for themselves. Since there were at least three women in Noriko's section who were competing for Tsukamoto's attention, she didn't feel like causing unnecessary tension by bringing up this violation of tea service practice. But lately the situation had grown worse. Now Tsukamoto left his tea cup in the sink after using it, and the woman who noticed it first would get up and wash it for him. He even expected Noriko, who was his senior by ten years, to serve him. Once when she called his attention to the rules, he appeared genuinely puzzled. He said he had never made tea in his life.

Tsukamoto looked perplexed, a tea cup in his hand. He had put it in the sink earlier, and when he was away from his desk for a few minutes, it came back, unwashed. This was the second time this had happened that day. He examined the inside of the cup carefully, and turned it upside down, frowning. Then he took it back to the sink. Everyone in the room pretended to be absorbed in their work and wouldn't lift their heads to watch him, but when he turned on the faucet and stuck his cup under the running water with a sullen scowl, several people looked toward Noriko. Tsukamoto put the clean cup into the basket next to Noriko's desk. "Well, well," he then said in a low voice, apparently intended for her ears. He seemed to know it was Noriko who had returned his cup to his desk.

"I don't understand why anyone would harass me like this," he continued in a voice that only Noriko could hear. Then he went back to his seat. For a while silence fell across the room and Noriko felt everyone staring at her, silently accusing her of once again giving someone a hard time.

The way Tsukamoto had washed his tea cup was awkward. He looked as if he'd stuck his hands into sulphuric acid. It was obviously true that he neither knew how to make tea nor how to wash a cup.

Noriko watched Tsukamoto talking on the phone, and suddenly her head became so heavy it was hard to hold it up straight. She didn't know why she suddenly couldn't stand looking at Tsukamoto's tea cup. Like other people, she'd ignored his behavior till then. Did it mean that she had come to the point where she couldn't bear seeing herself tied to her accounting books day in and day out without any chance of promotion? Was she comparing herself to Tsukamoto, who was cheerful and full of confidence? She knew her inferiority complex was surfacing again. She tried to tell herself she had a right to be more confident, but she couldn't convince herself. She kept staring at the drops of water on the bottom of Tsukamoto's tea cup.

It was later that night that Sugio came to her door, looking a bit depressed.

"Are you free next Saturday?" he asked shyly, looking more serious than she had ever seen him before.

"Here," he said, taking two tickets out of his breast pocket. "I bought more than I could use. They say it's a good movie, and I thought you'd like to see it."

"Both of them?"

"Well, one is for me. I wondered if you could go with me." They were advance sale tickets of a movie Noriko had wanted to see.

"Thank you, but I have to work late some Saturdays. If I can't go, it'll go to waste. Perhaps you ought to give it to someone else."

"I don't know anyone else I can give it to," he said and pushed a ticket into her hand. "I had a dream that I had an accident. I'm more cowardly than I thought. I had to laugh at myself in the middle of the night," he said, scratching his head.

Noriko wondered if he felt lonely because of his dream and wanted to see a movie with someone. She hadn't expected this weakness in Sugio.

"There was a time when I rode a motorcycle around, showing off how fast I could go. So I understand those guys. That feeling of having a close call, like when I almost lost control steering and nearly hit a pedestrian. My body remembers it, you know. Once a girl riding with me got hurt. It wasn't a serious accident but I was scared. I thought she might follow me around and nag me for as long as she lived."

"Did she follow you around?"

"No. I wasn't popular with girls. She told me she'd never ride with me again. I felt relieved, actually."

Somehow the time and place they'd meet before the movie on Saturday was decided. As she turned the key to lock the door behind Sugio, Noriko heard him whistling. When she realized she was about to hum the melody she'd just heard on the other side of the door, she hurriedly picked up the evening paper and spread it in front of her.

Traffic accidents didn't upset Noriko. They were just a part of daily life, she told herself. Even major incidents or big accidents would stop being newsworthy if they happened every day. The newspaper articles reporting them would then appear to be making news events out of nothing. The pages packed with tiny letters would start to look wasteful.

It wasn't fair for her to criticize Sugio or Tsukamoto for their audacity, Noriko thought. She realized that she herself found accidents reported on the paper dull most of the time, and that she looked for those that seemed more exciting and read them as a form of relaxation.

In her lifetime of thirty years, Noriko had never witnessed a scene in which blood was spilled. A few people close to her had died in unusual ways, but by the time she'd arrived at the death scene the bodies had been taken away and the aftermath of the accident had been cleaned up. Only various facts associated with the deaths, much more than she could handle, were left with her.

"An Escapade At High Noon: Two Cows Arrested In Factory" read the headline of an article. Even though she wasn't paying attention, it caught her eye. A comic caption, she thought at first, but she soon realized that it had been the factory's name and the district where it was located that had caught her attention.

There was a slaughterhouse behind this particular factory, and two cows, having escaped from the truck on their way to the slaughterhouse, had to be chased all over the grounds. No one knew how to calm the cows. The cows didn't know where to go. Factory workers chased the beasts around the grounds for three hours until finally a policeman who knew how to deal with cows arrived. This was the content of the article.

Noriko imagined the cows running around inside the factory's dark fence. When she was a little girl, cows and horses were led into this slaughterhouse; as they moved slowly, they dropped their excrement. Neighborhood children followed them, shouting such words as "dog killer," "cow killer," "horse killer." Noriko folded the section she'd been reading and threw it on top of a pile of old papers.

Most people have one or two memories they'd rather not think about; one of Noriko's was related to the neighborhood where this factory was located. Like a dark shadow that cuts across the light, this memory stood in her way, blocking her ability to see herself as a perfectly normal, cheerful person.

The corner of the factory where the two cows had run, sensing their impending doom, was where Noriko's father had died. That had happened eighteen years ago. No sooner was this recollection brought to consciousness than another, an offshoot of the main body, suddenly came back to her. "My first and last kiss," she said to herself.

The incident happened when she was in either fourth or fifth grade. It took place on the same road where the two cows ran, in the darkness of the factory's shadow.

One summer day near dusk Noriko was sent to the store for something needed to prepare dinner. On her way back she was stopped under the railroad bridge by a young man. The man came toward her, wearing a white shirt without a tie, slouching a little. The bridge was too low for an adult to walk under standing upright. Cars were rarely seen in this neighborhood; seeing someone who didn't live there was also rare.

"I wonder if you could tell me . . ." the man said to Noriko, smiling. "Do you know what 'baiser' is?" Noriko didn't know what to say. She shook her head.

"If you don't, I'll teach you."

A moment after she'd seen the smile on the man's face,

darkness spread over her and she couldn't see. Then something covered her mouth. She was overcome by a nasty, slimy sensation. The man's face was hanging over hers. She pushed him away as hard as she could and ran, hearing a loud laugh behind her.

When she got home, she found that she was holding what she'd bought at the store tightly in her hand. She washed her face and rinsed her mouth many times. And yet she didn't know exactly what had happened. When her mother asked if she had run all the way, Noriko nodded nervously without a word. Her heart went on pounding hard for a long time.

Nowadays, any ten-year-old girl would know about kissing, but Noriko had never heard the word "kiss," not to mention "baiser." There were no television sets or girls' magazines in her house to teach her. For awhile after this incident, Noriko was overly conscious of her lips when she ate or talked; she was afraid they'd start to rot. Still she didn't tell her parents what had happened. She understood intuitively that the incident was something shameful. Noriko wondered skeptically many years later if her difficulty in relating to men somehow had its roots in this experience.

A bag of memories is not as sturdy as one might think. A small rip from an insignificant newspaper article quickly becomes large enough to expose the bag's contents.

When she was a child, Noriko lived in a company housing project near the factory where her father worked. She lived there for eight years until his death, and for another three years after that in a smaller, uglier unit while her mother worked. It was in a soot-filled neighborhood along the River Sumida. A slaughterhouse, a filtration plant, a paper mill, and a factory that manufactured liquid ammonia lined the riverbank, with small houses scattered here and there between them. Depending on the direction of the wind, a variety of bad odors filled the air. In the spring, horsetails and other weeds covered the riverbank along the railroad tracks.

The chimney where yellow smoke escaped day in and day out was part of the factory. People used to say touching this yellow smoke would make you sick. There was a sign with a picture of a skull that said "No swimming" on the riverbank where children played. Watching people swim despite the sign was one of the ways Noriko and other children passed their time. In six years three children had fallen into this river and drowned.

There was hardly any other place where children could play safely in the neighborhood crowded with factories, shipyards and coal stations. So they often went to the pier by the shipyard and played there, jumping from one small boat to another. They'd play hide-and-seek in the coal bins, or put their ears to the rails and try to hear trains approaching. Compared to these activities, an incident such as being kissed by a stranger, however unpleasant, was far less dangerous.

It wasn't only the children, however, who were close to danger. Her father was killed in an accident; his body was torn in the kettle used to recycle papers. It happened the spring before Noriko entered junior high school.

Noriko didn't get to see the body of her father. The closed casket was put into the oven and cremated without her seeing the inside. The way the coffin bearers carried the casket made her wonder if they were just pretending; perhaps her father was not inside, perhaps he had gone off somewhere by himself. She had wanted to try carrying the casket herself, but she wasn't able to leave her mother, who sat and stared at the casket wordlessly.

The low land along the River Sumida where Noriko had grown up was filled with mystery and danger, but among the memories of her childhood she had pushed the manner of her father's death back into the depths of her mind.

Every day a huge amount of used paper was brought into the factory, where it was processed for recycling. Among the piles of paper were railroad tickets and, once in a while, some coins. Small coins collected at the railway gates were often discarded along with tickets, the total amount of which was not large enough to spend extra time counting. The papers were all put into a big kettle, but at the end of the process the coins would remain at the bottom. After the paper was liquidated and sent on to the next process, the kettle would stop for a while. During those five minutes or so, the man in charge of the kettle would leave the room, and workmen would crawl inside the kettle to clean; the "refuse" they tried to remove, of course, was coins. They knew the danger, but nonetheless went inside where sharp blades formed the shape of a wheel.

One day this wheel started moving while Noriko's father was still in the kettle. No one knew whether the switch was turned on by mistake or something went wrong with the machine. The formal report of his death stated that the accident was caused by his inattentiveness, that he was dragged into the machine. It would be too embarrassing both for the company and for the other workers to reveal the true cause of his death. After Noriko learned how it had happened, she had nightmares. In her dream her father screamed with his arms stretched up high as he tumbled around in the kettle among pieces of old newspapers and ten-yen coins. Since she had never seen the kettle she couldn't envision the scene very clearly while she was awake, but at night her dreams were vivid and clear.

Noriko had no idea that her father had been risking his life every day for coins that amounted to as little as one hundred yen. She wasn't aware that her family was poor. After all, there were children around her who collected junk instead of going to school, and some of her classmates were absent for many days because their parents couldn't pay for school lunches.

The kids who lived in the same company housing as Noriko teased her. "Your dad was a slowpoke," they said. "He was slow but wouldn't give up. My dad is mad at him. 'Cause of him, other guys can't have extra pocket money now. That's what my dad says."

By connecting bits of information, Noriko learned the truth about her father's death. No one blamed him for risking his life for small amounts of money, but they scorned and criticized him for being slow, for misjudging the time it took to get out, and for exposing their secret activity.

The children were even crueler to Noriko after her mother started working at the same factory in the section where paper was sifted. "Your ma picks all of the coins before she sends the paper to the kettle. Is she trying to revenge herself or something?" the children said. They were probably right. The men, who were now prohibited to clean the kettle, had lost a source of pocket money.

"I don't mind quitting school. I'll go to work," Noriko told her mother one day. It wasn't necessarily out of sympathy; she couldn't bear the bad mood her mother always seemed to be in. Noriko was in the seventh grade then, and her mother, who'd grown bitter toward the people living in the company housing, repeatedly told her daughter that she wanted to save money and move.

"Junior high is a compulsory education. It's my duty to make you go to school. I doubt there's a single parent who doesn't feel the way I do. Besides, your father wanted you to go to college," she said. She smiled as she smoothed her lusterless hair. It was rare in those days to see her smile, and the way she talked reminded Noriko of her father.

Noriko's father had been different from most of the other men in the neighborhood, who went outside in their underwear and abused their children. He was a quiet man, and when he was home he sat with his back straight, reading mystery novels. He wouldn't take his trousers off to relax even in summer.

As time went by, Noriko's father slowly became a part of her past she didn't want to remember, and consequently, she and her mother had little to talk about. When Noriko graduated from junior high school her mother quit her job, and they moved out of the company housing into an apartment. After that her mother worked cleaning office buildings, until she died of cervical cancer. The last ten years of her life were more comfortable since Noriko, having finished high school, worked as well.

Whenever Noriko tried to persuade her to quit working, her mother said, "When you get married, I'll have to go back to work anyway." Her face, which by then had frozen into a look of stubborn stoicism, would soften momentarily. "If I work until I retire, I'll get a pension and that'll be enough to feed myself. There's no reason I should quit now. My body's used to working."

She died before she could retire.

Noriko's mother was thirty-five or -six when her husband died, only a few years older than Noriko was now. Her uterus slowly developed a cancerous lesion which eventually took her life. Was that female organ, which must have seemed like an unclaimed lost object, only a nuisance to her mother? Noriko wondered.

Ever since she found herself left alone, Noriko experienced moments when she felt unconnected to the rest of the world, swinging back and forth like a thread hanging in the air. The upper end of the string was hidden in the clouds, making it impossible to see what it was tied to, while the other end hung in midair, left to the mercies of the wind. Although she didn't find this situation particularly uncomfortable, it made her feel unstable. She thought the sky would be less cluttered if a gusty wind blew the hanging string away.

It wasn't only her mother who had disappeared from Noriko's world. The neighborhood where she had grown up had also vanished without a trace, making it difficult for her to track her memories. She had heard that within a year of her and her mother's departure the company housing was remodeled into a concrete four-story building. The apartment building where they had lived for ten years was also torn down; as soon as Noriko left it after her mother's death, it was rebuilt into a pale blue modern building, transforming itself from a cheap clapboard apartment into a trendy condominium.

After her father's death, Noriko and her mother were able to afford only an old, run-down apartment; it wasn't easy to find new apartments in those days. Most houses, hastily built and clustered together, quickly rotted, as if trying to escape from human use. Except for the main road where the streetcars ran, the neighborhood was full of narrow, winding roads; the alleys and eaves of the houses always looked dirty, not only because of the ever-present soot, but because they were so old. It was fortunate for the poor, nonetheless, that there were a few old, half-rotted apartments left here and there.

Time passed and the clusters of shabby dwellings disappeared. Now the news of people suddenly dying or being killed on a road was commonplace—a time when runaway cattle became a newspaper item and the death of humans didn't. Having worked in an office for over ten years, safe from life-threatening situations, Noriko felt she was no longer the uncomplicated, unclouded being she had been as a child. Her dull-colored eyes looked longingly for something, but she couldn't see her reality clearly. There had been a time when she, too, felt immune from physical danger, poverty and anxiety about the future. That time, however, was unfairly short. She had learned to be suspicious early on: whenever she saw neighbors talking, she thought they might be laughing at her father. Did that short stretch of time alter her personality? she wondered. She knew that her life now was ordinary and safe, and yet she feared something. The surrounding environment of noise and cheerful moods seemed only to reinforce her sense of danger. She couldn't see into the people around her because of the loud colors assailing them from outside. Newspapers told her that some people lived dangerously, risking their lives, and such people were full of mystery to her.

She tried to draw a mental picture of her father's face, something she hadn't done since her mother's death. She longed for him, a man with a faint smile on his face quietly sitting with downcast eyes, reading a book. When she pictured his face he seemed to be telling her that he was happy about the way he had died.

Nowadays no one can die like he did, Noriko thought. She wanted to believe that through his ghastly and ugly death her father obtained a right, as it were, not to let anyone else die in such a violent fashion. In contrast people would die from motorcycle accidents, she thought; it would be impossible to eliminate motorcycles altogether even though people died riding them.

Noriko's father had stepped into the kettle after other more efficient workers had left, knowing that the wheels could start any minute. He must have always been a few minutes behind other people. It wasn't just that day. He was naturally slow, but then again he confronted danger more bravely than other men. The suspense he had felt at that moment was buried somewhere in the pile of dust, never to be experienced by anyone else, safe in an off-limits zone.

His daughter, however, was ashamed of the way her father had died, and she learned to say that it was just an accident when people asked about him. When she got used to dealing with the question, she also learned to smile a bit. She knew her smile would give the impression that she was bravely facing her cruel fate. Meanwhile, the words she wanted to spit out were stuck inside her, and eventually rusted away. She thought her memory of her father had also decayed and died along with them.

Noriko had always felt that her personality, particularly her shyness, was passed on to her by her father; she had accepted it as part of her destiny. Not only his mediocrity but his shameful death was a part of her fate. But now his face, emerging out of memories stirred by the newspaper article recounting the cows' escapade, was filled with radiance. Unlike the people around her who she didn't care about, her father had such vivid coloring and substance that she thought he might somehow respond if she spoke to him; he seemed to be smiling at his mediocre, timid daughter. But Noriko felt frozen and hard, like a fossil. She couldn't find the words with which to address her father.

When he arrived in the morning, Tsukamoto went directly to the place where the tea cups were kept. Finding his own cup, he said in a loud, cheerful voice: "Who wants tea?" A few people raised their hands and Tsukamoto put several cups on the tray without bothering to find out whose they were. When he'd done this much, his boss called and he trotted off, leaving the tea cups and the pot of hot water behind.

"I wish I could relax once in awhile and have a nice cup of tea," he muttered on returning. He poured tea into his cup and, forgetting about the others, started drinking. Before he finished his tea there was a telephone call for him and on his way back to his desk he put his tea cup in the sink. The moment she saw this Noriko stood up abruptly as if by reflex; she went to the sink, grabbed the cup Tsukamoto had just left, and put it back on his desk.

Noriko suddenly saw her father's wry smile and heard his voice addressing her. "He's a capable guy, isn't he?" her father said. "He is, and he's got a large wing to fly with," she answered. "You're jealous, then." "You might say that, Father, but that's not all. What I want to do is to clip the tip of his wing and put it on my shoulder. Just thinking of it makes me itch." "Don't get too excited, or you'll make a mistake. You're not the type who can handle so many things at once. Look at me. Being a stickler, I lost my life." "I know, but still I want to make that man wash his tea cup. You'll see how stubborn I can be about trivial things."

Noriko tore a sheet from her pad and wrote down a few words: "Wash your own cup. That's what everyone else does here." She took the paper and put it under Tsukamoto's tea cup on his desk.

"Well, I see you've been sort of. . ." began Tsukamoto. Noriko was getting ready to leave. He looked agreeable and bowed a little, scratching his head.

"Do you think I've been harassing you?" Noriko asked, as she went on clearing her desk.

"You must've thought I was stuck up or something. I appreciate what you've done for me," he said, looking at Noriko intently and making her uncomfortable.

"Would you like to go for a drink with me sometime?" he continued. "I'd like to treat you to show my gratitude."

"I can't drink alcohol."

"I feel I have to do something to make it up to you, though," Tsukamoto persisted, narrowing his eyes. "I know an interesting spot, and there you'll find out what women are really like. It'll be good for you, I'm sure. You shouldn't be so square, you know. Do you feel inhibited?" he went on, murmuring and coming close to her, still smiling. "How about next Saturday? I'll keep that evening open."

Noriko stared back at him for a moment; she couldn't believe what she'd just heard.

"I have something to do next Saturday," she said.

"Are you afraid? It's a good opportunity for us. I didn't think you were that timid," Tsukamoto said, keeping up his amiable and friendly manner.

"I think I'll be free after ten," said Noriko in a stiff voice, giving him the name of the coffee house where she was to meet Sugio that day. She said to herself, I've no intention of being there, of course. But on the other hand, I might show up with Sugio after the movie.

"It's settled then. I hope you'll keep your word. I'm the type who gets very upset when stood up by a woman," said Tsukamoto. As he walked back to his desk to finish his work, Noriko saw he'd returned to his usual self: an able, good-natured staff member. Rather than being shocked at his quick transformation, she was impressed by his toughness.

That energy in men—who pursue wars, create orders and construct neon-filled cities, and who boast of their accomplishments—must come from this toughness, a quality her father lacked, she mused. The reason she was able to stomach Tsukamoto's aggressiveness was because Sugio had asked her to go to a movie. No matter how insignificant it was, his invitation bolstered her. Without it she probably wouldn't have been able to control herself and would have lost her temper with Tsukamoto. Yet she knew that the brazenness Sugio had shown when he borrowed her newspapers stemmed from the same mentality Tsukamoto possessed. They're all the same, she thought. Her father's quiet smile had no power to diminish the force of Tsukamoto's rudeness. Walking faster than usual down the darkening street afterward, she didn't feel like going back to her apartment; she felt a strange fear slowly mount inside her.

If I refuse to let him read my newspaper, will he get upset? Noriko wondered. What will Tsukamoto do when he finds out he has been stood up? Will he come to my apartment? What will I do then? Will Sugio come out of his room to rescue me? She suddenly felt shaky, as if there was no solid ground under her feet.

Blades of a big wheel quietly wait for the switch to be turned on. A kettle that eats a human. Unable to forget the taste of a sacrificial lamb, it waits patiently for the next victim.

If I go back to my apartment now, she said to herself, I'll have a hard time resisting going to Sugio's room with the excuse of bringing over some newspapers. She stood still for a moment in the midst of the crowded train station, bewildered by the severe expressions on the faces surrounding her. I can't let them see my weakness, at least not until ten o'clock next Saturday, she thought. She put her rail pass back in her pocket and studied the map above the ticket booth. With three transfers she could get to that sooty town along the river. It won't take more than two hours, but still it'll be close to midnight when I get back to my apartment, she thought.

Yet she decided to go. She suddenly felt light on her feet, and they started moving of their own accord, carrying her in the opposite direction of her apartment. She slid onto the train just before the door closed, inviting a scolding from the conductor.

Although she'd lived her entire life in the same city, Noriko had gone further away from the river each time she moved. Each time she felt the neighborhood where she had grown up disappearing, slowly disintegrating behind the main streets. As she became used to seeing new buildings and modern houses going up, she found it harder to believe that the dreary neighborhood with its maze-like alleys still existed.

It doesn't matter whether it's still there or not, thought Noriko. From the train she saw brightly lit streets that seemed to stretch endlessly. But was there any way she could defeat Tsukamoto without help? she wondered, putting thoughts of her old neighborhood away. Heading toward the place where she had left all of her troubling memories she was reminded of her urgent, unsettled present reality. I've certainly accumulated more than a few memories, she thought. As if she believed she could keep reinventing her life, she had allowed herself to make her present life unbearable. As if she had plenty of time to start a new and different existence.

One way to get even with Tsukamoto would be to become a capable employee herself, to be even more able than he was. Another way would be to make herself attractive to him as a woman so he'd feel intimidated. This seemed a quicker solution. There was a third way: she could be a tough, hard-nosed career woman who would harass younger colleagues to the point where people become disgusted with her. Or, she could simply be a good-natured but totally insensitive type. This last approach was possible only on the condition that she didn't mind hurting herself in the process. But suppose Tsukamoto left his tea cup in the sink again tomorrow? What would she do then? Just imagining that possibility made her so upset that she felt hot. She would probably throw the cup and let it smash into pieces.

What about seducing Sugio into marrying her? Then she could quit her job. Noriko couldn't help smiling at this idea. I'm the one who's taken in, she said to herself, thinking these silly thoughts. But if Tsukamoto and Sugio got into a fight over me, could I remain aloof? What then? The scenarios she created all seemed unrealistic and silly, and yet she dwelled on each of them quite seriously, imagining various strategies. She found she was enjoying herself.

Suddenly a black shadow crossed her sight. The scene in

front of her was now divided into two sections by a black belt where there was no illumination. It was the river.

Noriko walked down the stairway, ready to see the dusty road which, in her memory, ran straight in front of the station. However, her vision was blocked by two rows of shops lined up one after another. Only when she passed the arcade with ten or so shops on each side did she find a familiar road. The space in front of the station, now covered by the arcade, didn't seem to be the same as she remembered. Certainly it had been much smaller. But there was the Big Bridge on her left, hanging over the dark river, arched exactly the way it was in her memory. And also the small police station by the bridge and the dilapidated restaurant with signs that said "Tasty And Nutritious." When Noriko saw this restaurant, which had looked run down twenty years before, her heart started pounding.

A fishing boat glided slowly under the bridge, causing ripples of black water. There were several smaller boats tied by the concrete bulwark. Since the railing was only as high as Noriko's hip, it would be easy to jump from there into the water. Three boys in their school uniforms were leaning against the railing looking into the water.

Noriko saw one of the boys climb up to the top of the railing and begin walking along its narrow ledge. The other two ran to the middle of the bridge. She went up to the boy on the rail and walked along with him slowly so she wouldn't startle him.

"I want you to stop what you're doing," she said softly.

"How come? It's none of your business," replied the boy, stopping for a moment.

"It's my business. I'm here, you see, and if you fall, I'll have to go for help."

"You don't have to. I won't fall," boasted the boy. Noriko wondered if this boy would act as Tsukamoto had the other day.

"Do you know there's a police station at the end of this bridge?"

"Yeah, I know. But I'll get off before they see me."

"How about if I push you?" Noriko said, extending her arm toward the boy's shoes. He stopped walking and stood still. The other two boys who were walking ahead turned around and looked back, wondering what was going on.

"Those two would run instead of helping you. I'll push you, and I'll run, too. What would you do, then?"

"Why do you want to push me?" The boy was nervous now.

"Get down, then. I don't care either way, but I can't stand wishy-washy attitudes. So, which way do you want to go?"

"You're crazy, you know that? Are you from the juvenile detention center or something?"

Noriko smiled and extended her hand toward him. He ignored her offer and jumped down in one agile movement. "What a crazy lady I've got here," the boy shouted as he ran toward his friends. They disappeared into the nearby park. It was a small park where the poet Basho's monument stood.

When she crossed the bridge Noriko saw the road that would lead her to the neighborhood with the many alleys running along the river. It was an area where several small lumberyards clustered along the winding alleys. Boards were stacked against the walls on both sides of the narrow road, making it barely wide enough for one person to walk along. The smell of freshly cut wood was the same as before. There had been a small shrine somewhere to the left, Noriko remembered. As soon as she thought of it, she found herself in front of the Kumano shrine. The shrine was said to house a guardian spirit of the Big Bridge, but its entryway, which was even narrower than those of the nearby houses, was sealed off. Looking inside through a crack in a sheet of wood, she was able to see a small, grey shrine. As she strained her eyes, Noriko felt her heart beating irregularly. It was hard for her to believe that a district like this, where nothing seemed to have changed in twenty years, existed in the middle of Tokyo.

It grew darker as she kept walking. Soon there were no more houses. She remembered a school, warehouses and the factory at the end of the alley. Not a soul was around. Only people with specific business would be out here in this alley at such an hour.

As she continued to walk, Noriko wondered why she hadn't seen the river yet; she had expected to catch a glimpse of it between the buildings. The steel factory and the coal storage building were gone, and the shipyard wasn't there either. Noriko turned into another alley that she knew would lead to the riverbank where the railroad track ran. But the river seemed to have been completely blocked off by some sort of concrete wall, and where there had been a row of shacks there was now a high-rise apartment building. Surrounded by the dark warehouses, the building was like a giant cluster of light. Noriko stared up at it, and a chill ran down her spine.

The apartment building had eleven or twelve stories. Well-lit, neatly lined-up windows with various colors of curtains illuminated the surrounding darkness. The railroad tracks were supposed to be on the other side of the building, but was there really a railroad here? Noriko's memory seemed to be failing; it seemed to be fading into the light in front of her. Nothing seemed to have changed around the factory, not the way the gates stood, not the color of the fence, and yet. . . . A dog was barking somewhere. When Noriko was a child, dogs were set free at night. There were many stray dogs then, and children didn't want to go out alone at night.

Noriko looked at her watch. She felt frustrated not being able to find the river and the railroad tracks. Soon the dogs would be set free. She walked quickly back toward the factory.

A floodlight by the storage door shone on the grey wall, which had once been white. As she approached the spot where there was no light at all, her feet seemed to move faster and faster. The sound of her shoes echoed loudly, and her long, skinny shadow made a strange pattern, chased by the light from behind. Noriko tried not to make any sound, not to spread her shadow over the ground. This is a part of the neighborhood where intruders feel uneasy, she thought. She didn't feel the nostalgia of a person returning home. The mysterious mazes seemed more perplexing than ever, as if they were surrounded by a fortress. This neighborhood had resisted the invasion of outsiders; the trendy shops and modern houses were unable to penetrate it. Or rather, had it been impossible for this neighborhood to change, to transform?

Did I really live in this ghostly neighborhood for over ten years and let it become a part of me? Noriko asked herself. What did I come here for now, and why am I walking like this and becoming frightened? When the row of warehouses ended suddenly and a cave-like dark space confronted her, Noriko felt she couldn't take another step. She could no longer hear the sound of water, and she couldn't hear the dog. Whatever she had longed for was either gone or hidden from her by fences, and things she would rather not see remained in front of her, like the weed that stretched its roots deep in the ground. Frightened, she stood motionless for a while. It was as if someone had splashed black ink in her eyes. She felt her body being sucked and melted into the darkness. Turning around, she saw the storage walls reflecting the dim light. But the beam of light was not spreading; it looked like something solid and hard. If I go further, there'll be no way back, she thought. Her feet seemed glued to the ground. The only thing I haven't seen yet is the factory, but I don't have to see it, she said to herself. Her fear was persuading her not to go forward, to retreat.

But what is this dark space? Noriko took a deliberate step with her eyes half-shut and her arms stretched in front of her, searching. When her foot touched something hard and rough, she pulled away. Then she felt the thing in front of her with her hands and kicked it with her foot. When she realized that she was touching a wooden fence, she felt better. She started walking slowly, guided by the fence. It seemed to be a tall, dark fence built along the winding alley. Unable to reach the top of it, Noriko couldn't determine how high the fence was. She should have come during the day or on a clear, starlit night, she thought.

But how is it possible that a dark cavernous space like this exists in the middle of Tokyo? Noriko wondered again. It was as if all the darkness that had escaped the neon-lit city had converged here. Why do I feel I need to reassure myself that my father died and I was born in this wretched place?

This darkness is flowing into the river, she thought. She tried to remember the color of the river but as she stared at the darkness in front of her, it became the river, the black, muddy water. As she walked further, making several turns along the fence, she felt the darkness around her lift slightly. At another turn, she spotted a light, several meters ahead, coming from the front factory gate.

Noriko had been walking along the fence surrounding the large warehouse where used papers were stored. She realized the map in her memory was wrong. In her memory's cartography, the location of the front gate and the fence was turned around—the key spot was reversed.

She turned around and peered into the stretch of shadows she had just passed through. There she saw a space filled with darkness even more intense than before.

When a Man Loves a Woman

Eimi Yamada

He won't make love to me again, and I'm unhappy. "Willy, we should do it when we've got a chance, otherwise we'll be sorry later," I say to him, sitting on the edge of the bed. Here I am trying to seduce a younger man, and I'm dead serious. He smiles without taking his eyes off the television, but there is no sign that he'll change his mind. That part of his body, covered by the sheet, won't rise up. Even though it is night he is wearing dark glasses, and as he changes channels with the remote control, he says, nonchalantly, "The woman singing with Robby Neville has a good figure." I feel hurt, but as a last resort I tell him that I want him to make love to me. I know I sound like a gigolo pleading his patron. He lowers his glasses and looks at me as if surprised to find me still there. "Go and do your work. A woman who doesn't do what she's supposed to is not my type," he says unsympathetically.

It's you who doesn't do what you're supposed to, I say to myself, biting my thumbnail. The taste of oil paint embedded in it reminds me of what I'm supposed to be doing and makes me feel miserable. My role as "urban artist" should have nothing to do with this comedy: begging a younger man to make love to me and being refused. It's true, right now I don't look as sophisticated as when I go to a party, nor as sexy as when I lie on the beach. The Haines T-shirt I'm wearing has paint marks on it and my hair, which I've just washed, is tied back with a string. Are bare feet and blue jeans so unenticing? I ask myself. Since I've nothing on beneath my T-shirt, he can slip his hand under and enjoy me easily if he wants to, and yet. . . .

At first, I seduced him half-jokingly, but now I become exasperated at my own words. "Fine, Willy Roy, don't regret it later," I say, standing up. "Fuck you," I mumble as I open the door. Willy Roy smiles and replies quietly, "You too, honey." I slam the door, making a racket. Since he arrived, I've lost control of myself and it pisses me off. I shove my hands in my jeans' pockets and enter my studio, and there I see my canvas, much of which is still unpainted, taunting me. I sit on the chair, still angry, and light a cigarette. A woman who can't forget about the body lying in the next room—people call this woman an artist. I laugh at this idea, forgetting for a moment that I am angry.

Frankly, I wasn't pleased when this young man, whom I'd met in Miami during my vacation, came to visit my apartment. I had a lot of work to do to meet the deadline set by my agent. Furthermore, I had no intention of getting involved with the dull boys one often finds on beaches. Willy Roy was one of those, and even though he, being black, had no need to brown his skin, he had strutted up and down the beach enjoying himself. One day when I sat at a bar at the edge of the beach, closing my eyes between sips of Gordon's gin with lime, he came over. Since I had just finished a canvas and sold it at my asking price, I was feeling good. I let him sit at my table.

He wore a white linen suit without a shirt underneath, tennis shoes without socks, and a Panama hat. He looked exceptionally dandy, but I was neither so young that I'd fall for this type of man nor so old that I'd want to take care of him. Not bad at all, but many resort beaches have this type, I said to myself as I watched him smoke a cigarette out of the corner of my eye.

He talked about himself in a leisurely way. It wasn't unpleasant to listen to his charming Southern accent. I ended up buying him a drink. Instead of thanking me, he smiled and stared at me. Underneath his dark glasses his eyes were very clear. A diamond in one of his ears flashed in the sun. A man like this is beautiful to look at, but that's all. . . .

"Do you want me, if I may ask?" he said. I thought I knew what was coming, and I said to him silently: Don't you dare take me for some small-town girl, or one of those rich, society women who hang around here. I like real country people, but I despise hicks who just can't make it in the city.

"Not at all," I told him and went back to concentrating on my own pleasures—the warmth of the sun outside the beach umbrella, the white sand, a good drink. I went back to congratulating myself on my accomplishments. To my surprise the man laughed happily.

"I like you," he said, making me choke on my drink. "I may fall in love with you."

"Are you with your lover?" he asked when I looked him straight in the face.

"No," I said, hesitating.

"And yet you handle yourself so elegantly . . . you are quite a woman, I can see."

I opened my eyes wide and looked at him. He didn't talk anymore but he kept smoking, his eyes fixed on the sea. After a while he stood up and shook my hand. "I'm so glad to have met you. Will you give me your address?" he said.

"What for?"

"It would be okay if I sent you a Christmas card, wouldn't it?"

I gave him my New York address, feeling slightly deflated. He carefully placed the small piece of paper in his wallet and made his departure. I gazed at the back of this beautiful young man, with whom I'd spent only an hour or so. As if he knew I was watching, he turned around and announced, "By the way, my name is Willy Roy Wilson. Don't you forget." Then he crossed the bar quietly, and walked out onto the beach. He didn't seem to be thinking about me anymore. It was already beginning to get dark outside. His linen suit looked pale orange in the dusk.

Willy Roy had made an impression on me, but it wasn't a strong one. Therefore when I answered the bell of my apartment, thinking it was my friend Angela, I couldn't tell who the man was standing in front of me, pulling up his coat collar, and saying how cold the New York winter was. I stood there in confusion, not realizing that it was the gigolo I'd met at the beach in Miami. Only when he removed his dark glasses in the same deliberate manner, and when I saw the diamond in his ear, did it come back to me. I recalled that strange hour from my vacation.

I invited him in. But as I was making coffee for the two of us, I couldn't help feeling completely confused.

"Why did you come to see me?" I asked. Willy Roy was putting large amounts of sugar and cream in his coffee; he looked quite comfortable in my nicely heated room.

"I came to deliver a Christmas card like I told you. I'm a bit late for that, though."

I couldn't believe my ears. I don't have time for this kind of impulsiveness, however perfect it might be for the place he came from, a nice, warm and easy-going climate. I have a deadline to make for a project which I've been working on for some time. If my agent and my sponsor abandon me, that'll be the end of me as a freelance artist.

"That's a nice painting. I didn't know you were a painter."

"It's not finished at all. You can see that, can't you? I don't know what you have on your mind but I haven't got any time to be fooling around with you."

"I didn't come to fool around with you. I have to go back to Florida in a few days. You do what you have to do, and I'll be quiet in the other room."

"The other room? You mean you're going to stay here? What will I say if my boyfriend drops by?"

"If a relationship breaks up because one doesn't see the other for a few days, it isn't worth keeping. You'd better break it off now. Tell him you've got to concentrate on your work and can't see him."

I didn't know what to say. There was something about him that made his words convincing. I told him he could stay for a few days on the condition that he leave as soon as he began interfering with my work. I also told him I had no intention of either looking after him or sleeping with him.

What would my friends think? Letting a guy you've met only once, practically a stranger, stay with you. But as I was hanging his coat in the closet, I began to think that such a sudden intrusion wasn't a bad thing. I needed some distraction. My work wasn't going very well, and the guy didn't look like a thief or a murderer. Besides, he was beautiful.

When I took up my brushes and palette knife, he disappeared into my bedroom with some magazines. He's quite reasonable, I thought. Feeling more accepting of him, I concentrated on my work, something I hadn't been able to do for quite awhile.

I worked hard for a few hours. Then, deciding to take a break and open a bottle of wine, I noticed a white envelope on the table. He really brought a Christmas card. So funny, I thought. I opened the envelope and found an ordinary greeting card. And then I read a line in his own writing which said, "And I am in love with you."

"What in the world is he thinking?" I mumbled to myself. I heard a knock at the door, and the very person who had delivered the Christmas card stuck his head in without waiting for my response.

"I wonder if I can use this bathrobe. I want to take a shower," he said, already wearing a blue bathrobe that belonged to my long-term boyfriend Mike. I threw the Christmas card at his feet.

"What's the meaning of this? Why should I be loved by you?"

He carefully picked up the card and looked at it contentedly.

"Looks nice, doesn't it? I'm not good at writing and so I did this very carefully."

"You say you love me but you've got no right telling me that."

"But I do have the right," he said calmly, pouring the wine I'd just opened into a glass. He looked at me as he sipped the wine. "I've told you I might fall in love with you . . . "

"Don't worry about me. I won't interfere with your work," he said as I remained silent, not knowing what to say. I'd forgotten I was about to take a break, and I picked up my palette, feeling annoyed. Why do this man's words sound so convincing when there's no basis for them, I wondered, squeezing some paint from a tube.

"I like your painting."

"Do you know anything about painting?"

"No. But this reminds me of the color of the sea we saw in Miami. This blue."

"This is not a landscape painting. It's an abstract, a person."

"I see. Then this is me, I take it."

I turned and stared at Willy Roy. He stood there smiling his cool, charming smile, the front of his robe drawn open. I saw it there, and quickly averted my eyes. I tried, with difficulty, to ignore the fact that he was standing there. I went back to my canvas.

I went on painting but my confidence was waning. Confidence and disillusionment are always warring inside me when it comes to my talent. When people applaud my finished work, I find myself a likeable person; when I paint in solitude, however, I often suffer from anxiety attacks and have to just sit on the floor, waiting for help. What help? Help from a God who would make me paint, I suppose. I don't think about God most of the time, but when I feel such helplessness, I want to put myself in the hands of something absolute. It is at such moments that I sincerely wish I were not an artist.

"You can't paint. Is that right?" Willy Roy was sitting next to me. I had no idea when he had come in. I had no energy left to say something stinging to him. I simply nodded. When he ran his hand through the hair hanging in my face, I didn't feel he was doing it as a prelude to a seduction. Then he brought the wineglass to my mouth. The wine traveled down my throat smoothly; it tasted good. But I still felt like a lost child. "Poor kid," murmured Willy Roy.

"I wonder why you can't paint? You're loved very much. . . ."

Willy Roy went on consoling me, and I realized that his words were what I wanted to hear. No one had ever talked to me with such tenderness. All I'd heard was that I was a talented painter. Contented with those words, I had never shown my loneliness to anyone until now.

When I came back to reality, I was underneath Willy Roy. Peeling my clothes off, he kissed me everywhere and talked in his sweet voice. He didn't offer the wonderful lies a man gives when making love to a woman. He talked about the cotton fields of his native North Carolina, and about his mother who hugged him after scoldings when he was a little boy. "Why do you talk so much?" I asked him between sighs. "Because we don't know much about each other," he said. Then he told me how charming the woman was who he saw sipping gin and tonic in the approaching dusk at that bar by the beach.

He surprised me by remembering our encounter with such detail: how my silk scarf was blown by the wind around my neck, how my lipstick was wet from my drink, and how he was aroused by my fingers when they squeezed a sliced lime.

We rolled on the floor, embracing and smearing our bodies with paint. And yet we were calm, and we made love leisurely. I sighed now and then but never cried out. He held me down by forcing my hands against the floor but was never rough. He kept talking and made me talk. Choking with pleasure, I told him how I sometimes became frustrated and anxious about painting. I told him how lonely I grew at times. I had never dreamt that I could talk like this to a stranger. I was making a confession, which until then my pride had always prevented. Now I was expressing my inner self, while reveling in this man's body.

There will be a painting on the floor, created by our bodies, I said to myself. It might be more beautiful than the one I'm putting on canvas because Willy Roy is making me feel this happy. My body, caressed by his words, painting. There was the red of wine spilled from the glass, and the pure white fluid coming from his beautiful body. As the two were mixed inside of me, it came out as hot rose, coloring my sighs. When I half-opened my eyes, his eyes greeted me, smiling. I tried to talk but darkness descended on me from the pleasure. "You can paint, I'm sure you can." I didn't answer and all I could see now through my half-closed eyes was his one diamond.

Willy Roy kissed me, made the sign of the cross in front of him, and said he wished my painting would go well. Then he left. I remained lying on the floor, with a cigarette in my mouth, lost in thought.

I couldn't explain what had happened. He had made love to me, I said to myself, and the way he had loved me came back with vivid clarity. How thoroughly he knew my body, I thought, blushing. How was it possible for him to discover so easily the many shades of every corner of my body, even those that were unknown to Mike? I was amazed at the fact that I had enjoyed such a pure sensation of pleasure, a sensation that I was able to reach only when I loved my body myself. And his words, which healed my ailing mind. . . . He had told me many times in the most natural manner that he loved me. I had never known a man so talkative, but he talked to me with genuine and smooth words. While we were making love, I learned about his family, his hobbies and friends, even the name of the high school he had graduated from.

What did I tell him? Perhaps only the story of my anxiety about painting. He hadn't learned anything about me. When I realized this, many things that I wanted him to know came rising up within me; I couldn't shut them out, and I got up.

I wanted to tell him first of all how his body had satisfied me. Had he been able to tell by my signals? When I dug my nails into his back, had he been able to tell how I adored his body, that it made me forget everything?

Why did I want to tell him these things? Perhaps I was grateful to him. And now I wanted to please him. Love must begin like this, I thought, and felt a bit embarrassed. Since painting had been the first priority in my life, I had chosen my boyfriends accordingly; they had to be mature, dispassionate types who would understand. In the past men had accepted my self-indulgence, and I liked them for that. I had never been eager to please the men I slept with, nor had I tried the common techniques most lovers use.

I peeked into the bedroom, not knowing what to do with myself. Willy Roy was sleeping, looking quite innocent with a pillow in his arms. Seeing the paint on his shoulder made me feel as though my heart was being squeezed. I stroked his cheek with the back of my hand, and he opened his eyes slightly, smiling at me.

"You go and work now. I'll wait here for you," he said. When I left the room, I felt like crying. As I picked the things up from the floor of my work room, I murmured to myself, "What should I do, I'm in love."

Now I'm miserable. I work for a while, and then I long for Willy Roy. I go to the bedroom, and he asks, "Have you finished your work?" I shake my head, and he tells me to go and do my work, as though he's my elder. I don't know what to do or say because I've never been turned down by men when I show an interest in going to bed. I go back to my work room and to my canvas. After a while, I find myself unable to sit still, wanting to be close to his body. I go to the bedroom again. He repeats the same question, and I give the same answer. He goes back to his newspaper or magazine, or turns the television on instead of making love to me. Finally, I give up and spend the rest of the night painting.

In the morning I'm totally exhausted but Willy Roy, who woke up early, brings breakfast to me. We eat it together, looking at my painting, which has shown some progress. He knows that I need to sleep now, and opens a bottle of wine.

The morning sun makes me feel so peaceful and comfortable that I no longer care for sex with Willy Roy. He is wearing his dark glasses (he says it's too bright), and sprinkles salt on my eggs. I sip my wine absent-mindedly, gazing at him as he butters my toast and pours ketchup on my hash browns. He tells me that I have to eat well, and I do as he says. He looks at me with satisfaction, and puffs his cigarette. He puts a record on, Percy Sledge, which I think he's too young to know. Then he assumes the air of a philosopher, and tells me that these precious moments are what make up our lives. I remember that the song is called "When A Man Loves A Woman." At the same time I begin to feel the effects of the wine. I can hardly keep my eyes open. Seeing this, he takes me to the bedroom. He peels my clothes off and I lie on the the bed, falling asleep with the feeling that, somehow, I've been tricked into this situation.

Once I threaten him by telling him that I can't paint unless he makes love to me. He ignores me and keeps on reading his book. My pride is badly wounded, and I grab the book from him and throw it away. When I start unbuttoning his shirt, however, he gives me a troubled look.

"If you go further than that, you won't be able to stop," he says, removing my hands from his naked chest, which I'd begun caressing. I feel embarrassed and can't do anything but stare at him. He, too, wants to make love. I know, because I feel the sign between his legs when I touch him.

Seeing I am about to cry, he tells me to come to him. I slip my body next to his and stay there for a while, not moving.

"If we make love whenever we want to, our relationship will be a mere diversion," he says as he gently strokes my hair.

He lifts my hand in front of his face and says with a smile: "That," nodding toward the canvas, "is more important than me when it has paint on it."

"If I didn't know your body, it would have been different. Why did you make love to me to start with?"

"I thought we needed some sort of beginning in order to love each other."

I leave the bed, unable to argue with him further. "He uses the word love too lightly," I murmur, going back to my work room, biting my lips.

One afternoon a few days later, we are in bed, half-naked, eating yogurt and watching television when Mike comes in without knocking. Dumbfounded, he stands there staring at us. I stare back at him, embarrassed. I don't even get out of bed, having decided in desperation that I don't care. Without hesitation, Willy Roy extends his hand to introduce himself, but Mike totally ignores this gesture and sits down on the edge of the bed, which shows no signs of being used for lovemaking.

"I want you to explain this," he says staring at me. He is angry but he is trying to be calm, perhaps because he notices that Willy Roy is younger than him. "You told me you were busy working and couldn't see anyone. And now you've got this young guy in your bed."

"We're not making love. Well, we did once but . . ."

"If you did it once, you'll do it again."

"No, that's not true," I say, starting to cry. Mike keeps staring at me in disbelief.

"If you want to, you can lie down, too. I guarantee nothing'll happen," says Willy Roy. Shocked at these words, Mike drops the cigarette he was about to put in his mouth.

"You . . . you're gay?"

"No, I'm not. I'm interested only in women. But as I've told you, I won't do a thing."

"You won't make love to her then? She likes sex, that I know. Or are you saying you can't do it?"

"I'm ready any time."

"He's really good, Mike."

"I love sex, too, but I also like to control myself."

Mike becomes more confused, and it seems that although he wants to get rid of Willy Roy, he doesn't know how. I don't know, either. What Willy Roy was saying was beyond us.

"I'm sorry, but I have to tell you this," Mike says. "She and I have known each other for a long time, and I believe I understand her very well. We also need each other."

"I have no intention of interfering in your relationship. I simply love her."

“Simply love her?”

“Is your dick big, may I ask?

“Of course it is.”

“Mine isn’t bad at all. I can show you if you want to see it.”

I see cold sweat on Mike’s forehead. I do nothing but watch, feeling the tension grow between them. I feel like laughing but at the same time I see that Mike is scared. It is Willy Roy who breaks the silence.

“Having sex doesn’t mean love. You can sleep with a woman just for fun, or to make money. You shouldn’t worry about our having had sex once, but you should be concerned about the fact that we’re in bed without making love.”

At Willy Roy’s words, Mike kicks a chair and opens the door, making a big noise. “Go to hell,” he shouts as he leaves. Both Willy Roy and I don’t know what to say for a moment, and then we burst out laughing.

“I made him mad, didn’t I,” says Willy Roy apologetically after we’ve laughed for a while.

“It doesn’t matter. We know each other well, so it’s okay.” I say and wipe the tears of laughter from the corners of my eyes. When I look up, Willy Roy kisses me on the cheek. He seems genuinely pleased and happy.

“I really like you very much. I have no problem finding women to sleep with, but I’ve been out of luck falling in love,” he says.

One day I’m awakened by a noise. Willy Roy is packing. I jump out of bed. He has already combed his hair and he is wearing his cashmere coat.

“Are you leaving me?” I ask.

"Don't look like that. We can see each other any time we want. I just came to deliver my Christmas card and stayed a bit too long." He smiles at me, sitting on the edge of my bed.

I go to the door with him, unable to decide whether I should beg him to stay. I am thinking many things at once: that he is too good a guy to let go, that I don't like to see myself act as if I haven't had much experience with men, and that there will be a chance to see him again. The thoughts swirl in my head. Willy Roy throws me a kiss as he walks out the door.

"When we meet again, we'll want to make love till we knock our brains out, won't we, baby," he says, looking back and pointing at me. He closes the door behind him, leaving me with the memory of his penetrating smile.

I go back to my work room, yearning for him, thinking that I want to make love to him one more time. Then I see my painting, which is finally finished. I can't help laughing in delight.

A Family Party

Hikari Agata

"Nisshinjiku." That's how Michi pronounces the name of this town where she was born. At one end of the town's cluster of high-rise buildings a new twenty-story structure called the Planet Hotel has been completed. Its interiors—the beds, the walls, the curtains—are all the color of ivory, but on the eighteenth floor there is a room with a black interior.

The floor is black, as are the walls and the frames of the screens. By the window is a black rectangular block with a grey telephone on it. Against one wall is a sofa bed with thin grey-and-white stripes. In the middle of the room is a large, low table, and on the table is a vermilion lacquered tray. Yūji and his brother-in-law Hiroshi, who is an architect, designed the interior, and I chose the throw pillows and the tray with the help of Kayoko.

My mother-in-law didn't say anything while she sat in the room and looked around. I had been worried that she wouldn't like the room with the black interior.

"I hope you like it," said Yūji. "Since we built the house in Yokohama in the traditional style to suit Dad's taste, we've designed this one differently."

"This is a nice room. Don't you think so, Michi?" said my mother-in-law to her granddaughter, rather than to her son. Six-year-old Michi was jumping on the sofa, where she'd gone straight from the door. "Uh-huh," Michi replied.

I felt relieved. I opened the shōji screen by the window. From the height of the eighteenth floor I could see West Shinjuku stretching out under the pale blue sky. Innumerable small houses crowded the entire view, and along the store-lined main highway I could see an unceasing line of cars. I saw three- and four-story buildings here and there, and a train was running between the houses. From this window, though, I couldn't see any of the high-rise buildings that towered up into the sky. I decided the room must be facing south. I remembered that from the window on the south side of the two-story house we used to live in I hadn't seen tall buildings either. Looking down from this height, however, I couldn't be sure about the actual direction.

I spotted a street on the right side that seemed to lead straight to our hotel. I turned around to ask if Kōta would come on this street and saw the faces of Yūji and Mother. I swallowed my words. "I'll go to the store now. Should I lock the other room, honey?" I asked instead, leaving the window. Yūji nodded, and Michi jumped down from the sofa, saying, "I'll come, too."

Leaving room 1801 I crossed the corridor and entered 1851, the room we reserved for Yūji's sister Kayoko, her husband and their son Masaru, who would soon be thirteen. There was no luggage in this ivory room, but I checked the inside anyway before I locked it.

Inside the descending elevator Michi made a sound as if she were blowing a feather, as if she herself were falling. I remembered a time when Kōta was three. He used to go into neighboring buildings and play inside the elevators. One day, gripped by fear for his safety, I packed a lunch and took him to the Central Park to spend the day. I repeated this routine until he entered kindergarten. On days when I woke up and heard the rain, I felt relieved because that day I could keep Kōta in the house.

In the lobby, there were several families with children who were taking advantage of the special price of 350 yen a night before the official opening. They were the stockholders, former landowners, and those involved in the construction of the hotel who had been invited to try out the rooms and see if everything was satisfactory. There were many children since school was out for spring break.

Outside the automatic door I stood looking around. The street seemed to have changed a great deal from the way I remembered it. I tried to look at the top of the building, which was decorated with white tiles, tilting my head all the way back until it started to ache. The building looked as if it was pushing into the sky. Michi also looked up, imitating me.

"Well, which way should we go?" I said, facing the street. "If we go right, we'll be on the big street and we can get to the station that way. If we go left, we'll have to go through those tall buildings but it'll also take us to the station. That way winds around a bit and takes longer."

Michi pointed toward the high rises. As I started walking with her, I thought about how, when the time came, I might tell my grandchildren about the hotel and its room 1801.

"Kōta was born in this town and we lived here until the beginning of his second year in school," I'd tell them. "When he was five, you see, people who wanted to build a hotel asked us to sell them the land where our house was. Your great-grandpa didn't want to do it because he'd inherited the land from his ancestors. He resisted until the end. But when other people had decided to sell their land, your great-grandma and your grandpa decided to sell, and then they persuaded your great-grandpa.

But they made it a condition that our family would have the right to use room 1801 as long as the hotel stands so that something would be passed down to you children. We had the right to decorate the interior any way we liked and to keep it for our use. So, you see, that room is our ancestral home in the sky, left for us by your great-grandpa."

There had been about twenty houses standing on both sides of that narrow street. I used to ride my bike to go shopping near the station. Coming back, I would cross the highway and take the road with small shops lining the left side; then I would turn to the left in front of the greengrocer. It was both sides of this road that were later turned into the building site of the Planet Hotel. A car scrapping plant stood on one corner, and our house was at the other corner. It was a two-story house with plastered walls and a sign on the front door that said: "Manufacturing: Cookie Molds." Beyond the opaque sliding glass doors was a small space paved with pebbles. There my father-in-law discussed work with his customers, and on a raised level next to it were his work bench and tool shelves, wood and some sheets of metal.

Next to us was a one-story wooden house where dry goods and cigarettes were sold; adjacent to this was a cafe with a brick façade, and next was a Western-style house with a bay window, which belonged to a legal scholar. I don't remember if the exterior was stucco or clapboard, but the ivy which blanketed the front of the house is still fresh in my memory. The land where these four houses stood, about 800 square yards, had belonged to the Tamiya family. Someone once told me that before World War II only the Tamiya house and the Western-style house had stood there among the trees and bushes.

The ground floor of the car scrapping plant had been a workshop and its steel structure was left bare; the owner of the business lived upstairs. In the small empty lot next to it were piles of old tires and car hoods. Adjacent to the lot was the Hori house, which was so old that removing one of its pillars would cause its total collapse. There had been an old-fashioned two-story apartment building right next to the Horis'. When the front door was left open, I used to be able to see the entryway with its shelves for shoes, the corridor, and a part of the stairway. The rest of the neighborhood buildings were small houses interspersed with small businesses: a store which sold comforters and blankets, a Chinese restaurant with at most six or seven chairs, a dry cleaner. They faced the street like hastily arranged building blocks.

From the beginning, this neighborhood had never seen large houses with fences and landscaped yards like those in the old residential area that had remained intact during World War II. This neighborhood had always given an impression of being disorderly. And yet, I was always relieved whenever I returned to it from the jungle of high-rise buildings. It had been a neighborhood where browns and greys melted nicely together, and the natural colors were gentle on my skin. There was a reason this neighborhood had been left without any newer and more modern-style houses: by the time such remodeling had become popular among the residents of Tokyo, the invasion of high rises was already in progress here, making people reluctant to invest in their existing houses and stores.

"Do you remember this street, Michi?" I asked my daughter. I used to walk her along this street in a stroller. But I knew she'd been too young to remember.

"We used to walk down this street a lot to go to Kōta's kindergarten." I told her that Kōta and I had given various tall buildings names such as "the hotel that reflects the sky," or "the hotel like a half-opened book."

"What's the name of that one?" Michi asked, pointing to a building with a wavy exterior. I didn't remember having given it a name; it must have been built after we moved three years ago.

"Well, it looks like an aurora, doesn't it?" I said, thinking of the days when I had walked this street with Kōta. He used to be able to tell exactly how many stories each building had.

I wondered to myself how Kōta was doing, since it took us over an hour to get here by car from our house in the suburbs of Yokohama. The traffic wasn't so bad but he was riding his bike. . . .

When Kōta had said that he wanted to ride his bike, I'd objected; it's too dangerous, I told him. His father, however, told him he could. They studied the map, marked the route with red pencil and measured the distance. And this morning at nine Kōta left the house on his bike with his lunch and water bottle. We left shortly after noon. According to the plan, he would arrive by three-thirty, or four at the latest.

"I wonder if Kōta's okay?" I said to Michi.

"He's okay," she replied.

Kōta was born a year after I'd moved to this part of town, and we lived here seven years. Yet I knew very little about this place beyond the triangular zone connecting the department store in front of the station, another shopping area, and the elementary school. But Kōta ventured much further, riding his kiddy bike. In Yokohama, too, he rides around the neighborhood to places I've never been. Once he told me he'd been to the industrial compound built on reclaimed land in Kawasaki.

When I was in junior high and lived in Suginami, this town was at the boundary of my map. I eventually graduated from high school and started working here, but at that time I knew only the busy shopping area on the other side of the station. And since my marriage I rarely go to that section.

My mother-in-law first saw me at the bank where I worked as a teller. She'd been trying to find a wife for her son, Yūji (he was over thirty then), and she asked someone to arrange the marriage. When I became her oldest son's wife and started living with her and her husband, she told me how much the town had changed. Yūji told me he used to see weasels in the neighborhood when he was a child.

The changes that I saw started with the appearance of Mr. Sawada and the other real estate agents. I remember it was on the day of Mrs. Hori's funeral. I was on my way to the Horis' to help with the cooking, and I saw two men in dark suits standing by the table under the tent where mourners were to be received. It was too early for the mourners to come, and I thought these men were relatives of the deceased. "Who has died, may I ask?" one of them asked as I approached.

Several days later the same two men came to the Tamiyas'. I was upstairs and didn't know about it, but Mother told me later. She said when they told Father of their plan to build a hotel, he curtly told them to leave, declaring he had no intention of selling the land his grandfather had passed down to him. Later Mother showed me an old account book with "Echigoya" written on its cover, and told me about the land the Tamiyas had owned.

Yūji's great-grandfather came to Tokyo from Echigo, and after a few years of apprenticeship with a rice merchant he was able to buy a store which he called "Echigoya," and with the money he saved he bought some land. When he died, the land in Nishi-Shinjuku was inherited by his daughter, and the store and the land in Jingumae went to his son. Perhaps this daughter didn't have too many expectations of the undeveloped land she had been given, since one of her sons was trained as a tailor and the other as an artisan who made cookie molds. The older son, the tailor, died in the war and his younger brother, my father-in-law, inherited the land. Though he was able to come home at the end of the war and resume his business, there wasn't enough flour and sugar to produce cookies, and Western-style sweets were becoming so popular that there was little demand for the molds he made to bake traditional-style cookies. Soon Yūji was born, but life was difficult. Black market stalls proliferated near the train station, and even the shabbiest house was easily rented. Rumor had it that if an empty lot was found people would go ahead and build a makeshift house overnight without bothering to get permission from the landowner. The Tamiyas decided to lease their entire property.

The land which the real estate developer had mapped out for building a hotel belonged to three landowners: the scrap dealer, the Tamiyas, and a man who owned several buildings near the train station. This man didn't live in the neighborhood, and he had already agreed to sell his land, leaving only the Tamiyas and the car demolitionist to be persuaded.

The scrap dealer ran his business with his son, who was my age and being trained by his father. As soon as the issue of selling the land was brought up it became apparent there were problems between the father, this son and his three brothers.

"You should hear them carry on," said the son's wife when she and her husband came over to our house. "My husband's brothers left because they hated their father's scrap dealing business, you know. Because of my husband, the business and the land stayed with us. It's unreasonable they insist on their rights now that . . . "

"I completely agree," interrupted her husband. "We should spend the money to buy you a diamond ring and a mink coat."

The first neighborhood gossip I heard when I came to live with the Tamiyas was about this scrap dealer's son. He was a short and ordinary-looking man, but his wife wore heavy makeup even early in the morning. I often saw her when I took garbage to the pickup spot near her house. She always wore fashionable clothes. Her father-in-law, who was unhappy about her spending so much time making up her face and so little time doing housework (she was careless about money too, it was said), once complained about her to his son and compared her to the greengrocer's young wife. The story goes that the son told his father, "For my wife I'd rather have a good-looking woman who just sits there than an ugly one who works hard."

Since I had never seen this woman without makeup on, it was difficult for me to tell if she was good-looking, but I thought the son's remark was interesting. The entire time I'd worked at the bank, I'd never encountered a man as frank as this. Soon afterward, I became better acquainted with the wife. When I got pregnant she, sounding envious, confided in me that she couldn't have a baby herself. And she was very good to Kōta.

"Mommy," called Michi, looking up. "Why are you mad and laughing?"

"What? I'm not mad."

"But you are."

"I was thinking, that's all. Do you remember the auntie of the car wrecking place?"

Michi tilted her head, then shook it.

"You don't? Then how about Misao, your piano teacher?"

"I know Misao."

"She gave you a teddy bear when we said good-bye to her, didn't she? We may be able to see her today. That'd be nice, wouldn't it?"

Shortly after I came to live with the Tamiyas, my mother-in-law told me to deliver rent increase notices to our tenants. After living with my mother in a civil servants' housing project until my marriage, I knew nothing of these things, and when I went to see the tenants I apologized, saying, "I'm really sorry about this." At the cigarette shop next door the old woman was tending the store. I felt guilty giving her the notice since the store didn't seem to be doing well. When I went to see Misao, who was still a music student at that time, her grandfather, the jurist, took the notice. He carefully read it in front of me, making me feel uncomfortable, as if I'd done something wrong. And Mr. Gotō, who had opened a cafe after quitting his job at a firm because of some personality conflicts, looked at me and said, "You've married well, haven't you?" There was a forced openness in his voice and I felt uncomfortable; it made me distrust him afterward.

By the time I came here the price of land was already too high to consider selling, and none of the tenants really thought of moving. Many people who had rented land right after the war had married and made their homes here, and it was here that their children were born. Most of the households were two or three generational, and I was called "the young Mrs. Tamiya." I quickly became involved in various neighborhood activities. I helped with the cooking whenever there were funerals, and when work was done on the sewer I took turns serving workmen at tea time. When it was our turn at the neighborhood association, I delivered poison to kill rats, collected contributions for the Red Cross, and distributed amulets of our neighborhood shrine, the Kumano Shrine.

On the day of the festival of the Kumano Shrine, which was at the far end of the Central Park, the empty space adjacent to the car wrecking yard became a place to serve sake and to return the portable shrine after it went around the neighborhood. Children wore black happi coats which the neighborhood association rented for them, and Kōta, with his nose powdered for the day, wore one too. Father, in the same yukata everyone wore, sat at the sake booth. Unlike the greengrocer, who was talking loudly, and the scrap dealer, who was acting important, Father sat in the corner smiling. He was one of the officers of the neighborhood association, in charge of the community storehouse where they kept an old fire engine and funeral paraphernelia. Uninterested in being the head of the association, he took the job of keeping the things in storage in good order.

Mother spent some of her time talking and drinking tea with the other women but Father didn't do anything except chat with his neighbors on the street. Not a man who enjoyed drinking, his favorite pastime was pachinko. Once in a while he took Kōta to one of those pinball game parlors in front of the station and they would come back with chocolate, his prize and rice cakes from the department store.

"This is the school your dad went to," I told Michi as we

passed the fenced school grounds across from "the hotel that reflected the sky."

"Did my brother go there, too?"

"He was supposed to, but he didn't. As the big buildings went up and people who had once lived around here moved away, there weren't enough children for the school. There were only three first graders the year your brother started school, and so he had to go to another one across the highway so he'd have friends, you see. There's no longer a school here."

"But there's a school," disagreed Michi.

"It's just the building but it's not being used."

"That's wasteful, " Michi said.

"You're right. That's why they're thinking of turning it into a school for the physically handicapped. Many streetcars pass by here, so it's a good location."

The year before Kōta was supposed to enter this school, its entire population was about the size of one class in other primary schools, yet there were seventeen teachers plus the staff, which included a janitor and lunch service personnel. This imbalance had been brought to the attention of the local assembly, and rumor spread that the school would soon be closed. When Kōta entered the school across the highway, the issue of selling our land had already been discussed. I couldn't admit this to the mother of Kōta's friend, Hiroshi, who had also chosen not to enroll her son in the school which was soon to be closed. By then problems had arisen between those who would receive a great deal of money if they moved out of the area, and those who were not landowners. This conflict destroyed the harmony among the mothers, who until then had felt they were equals in every respect. Unfortunately, sometimes the children were embroiled in the problems of their mothers.

When we moved to Yokohama, I didn't tell anyone there that we built our house from the money we were given for selling the land. I knew all our new neighbors carried heavy mortgages for their houses, and I was sick of hearing about owning and not owning land, the size of houses, and so on. Fortunately the mothers in my new neighborhood were occupied with the activities that went along with living in a suburban development. They founded a children's club and a library, and started a street market where they could buy vegetables directly from nearby farmers. All this was possible, I thought, because they were still young.

Most of our family gradually made friends in our new neighborhood, both with newcomers like us and with those who had been there before us. My father-in-law, however, having left behind the environment in which he'd lived for so many years, seemed lost. Knowing that he cared more about his work than his relationship with his neighbors, we thought that as long as he could continue his work he would be happy. We were wrong. It was a different situation with my mother-in-law. She often complained about my leaving home so much, but I thought it was probably good for her to deal with such things as shopping on her own in a new neighborhood.

Father's dementia started soon after we moved to Yokohama. He began loitering in the neighborhood. All of the work around the house was just about done by then and the children became used to their new environment. I told Father about my work with the other mothers organizing a children's club, and I tried to spend time with him taking walks. Between Mother and I we tried not to leave him alone in the house. He seemed to improve for a while, and he started teaching the children how to make bamboo dragonflys and tops. Since he had regained his spirits a bit, Mother and I let our guards drop. Then one day he began walking aimlessly on the street that leads to the highway. He was hit by a car. He died before he got to the hospital. Although we talked about his death as a consequence of his dementia, we knew he had been feeling guilty for selling the land he had inherited from his ancestors. We hadn't discussed it, but we knew it in our hearts. Even so, what could we have done?

The streets in front of the department store on Saturday afternoon were full of people.

"There're so many people in Tokyo," I said.

"Are there a thousand?" Michi asked.

"There are more."

We went into the basement of a department store where they sold food and bought sushi and pickled vegetables, like we used to when we lived here.

Living in our new neighborhood I miss the convenience of shopping for food prepared by the well-known old stores. Instead, in Yokohama, I have learned to enjoy picking edible grasses, like magwort, with Mother, and making cakes or pickling them. Mother discovered magnolia and dog sorrels not far from the house. She makes sushi wrapped with magnolia leaves and cooks young dog sorrel shoots. She started doing this six months after Father's death. Until then she had spent much of her time in a daze.

"He couldn't do a thing for himself," she had said. "I didn't know anyone who needed more help than he did. When he's gone I'll be able to do all kinds of things, I used to think, but now there's nothing I feel like doing." When I saw her starting to pick grasses and leaves as if she were trying to forget about Father, I couldn't help worrying about her.

"Shall we go back the other way?" I asked Michi as we left the department store, where I'd bought the kind of rice cakes that Father had liked so much.

"Kōta should be here soon," I said to Michi.

"How about Masaru and Auntie Kayoko?"

"They've probably arrived already."

At the time everyone had said, "It would've been so much better if this issue of land hadn't fall upon us." Although Father had declared at first that he wouldn't sell his land, our fate seemed decided when the Chinese restaurant owner agreed to sell. "The agreement to sell by one of the owners who has the most land means that the sale is pretty much decided," Yūji had said. He had been doing a great deal of investigating about the sale of the land.

"It's eighty and twenty, they say," Mother reported to me that day, coming back from her shopping. She was pale and couldn't stop shaking.

"What do you mean eighty and twenty?" I asked her.

"You've heard about tenants' rights, haven't you? That means eighty per cent of the money goes to the tenant, leaving the landowner the rest, twenty per cent. Mr. Gotō and the cleaner told me just now. Even if we agree to sell the land, we'll get only twenty per cent of the money."

That night when Yūji returned from work Mother repeated what she had heard. Yūji said, "That seems to be the case."

"Do you mean to say that what we thought, that we had

land worth ten million yen, is wrong? We'll get only two million even if we sell the land?" Mother asked.

"It'll be Father who decides," Yūji finally said. It seemed painful for him to say this. "He has to have some information in order to make the decision, and so I consulted with Hiroshi," he added. Father was listening without a word, with his head down.

"What'll happen if we insist on not selling?" Mother asked anxiously.

"Apparently, the scrap dealer has agreed, too. Only there are some unresolved issues like the land he'd get in replacement. It'll take some time to get everything settled, but if he's really made up his mind, we'll be the only ones left. And even if they change their plans and build around us, we'll be right next to the high rise. I've heard about cases where gangsters pressure people and give them a real bad time."

"If such a thing happens, it'll be bad for Kōta and Michi," said Mother, sighing.

Although Yūji told us we should think it through and take as much time as we needed, what was actually left for us to do was to wait until Father decided. Kayoko and her husband Hiroshi came to join the family discussion, but Hiroshi, an architect, made his position clear from the beginning. "I've given all the information I have to Yūji," he said and declined to participate. He probably didn't want to say anything that might give the impression he was in favor of selling. He and Kayoko had bought a condominium in Setagaya five years earlier and they were paying the mortgage on it. The elder Tamiyas had given them money at that time, but not having much cash, what they were able to do was limited.

"I really don't like this situation," said Kayoko.

"We're doing fine on our own. If we say Dad shouldn't sell, then I feel we're being irresponsible, but if we recommend that he sell, that'll make us look like we're expecting our share. It's so difficult for us, you see. I do think the four of you should decide yourselves. That'll be fine with us, really. You can see why Hiroshi doesn't want to say anything, can't you?" Kayoko said openly. I knew there'd be no end to this mess if we started interpreting one another's intentions maliciously, or if we tried to manipulate each other.

Before we reached a decision, the tenants who leased the land from the largest landowner started moving. The first to move were the Horis who lived next to the car yard. Mr. Hori had worked as a security guard for several years after his retirement from a civil service job, but when I came to this town he wasn't working anymore. He had a square face and was generally unsociable. He wasn't pompous though, and he impressed me as an honest old man. The issue of the land sale began right after his wife's sudden death from a stroke. His daughter and her family had come to live with him but she and her husband worked and their only child, a son, was in high school. They'd lived there less than a year before they moved away. I could understand why they left. The house was so old that it looked as if it would fall apart any day. But Mr. Hori had lived in this house for a long time, carefully repairing things here and there.

From one of our upstairs rooms I could see the roof of Mr. Hori's house, which had several new slates among the old ones. I used to get nervous whenever I'd see him on the roof or on a ladder, fixing the siding of the house. But Mrs. Hori would always be down below, watching her husband attentively and talking to him. I would often see them in the department store walking together through the food counters as if they were just taking a stroll. They seemed to be a nice old couple who got along well.

A week or ten days after Mr. Hori moved away with his daughter's family I saw someone by the entrance of his house. When I looked more carefully, I discovered that it was Mr. Hori, standing on a plastic beer case, stretching his arm up to reach the top of the sliding door, scraping at something. For a moment I wondered if he was repairing the house in which he no longer lived. I stood nearby and watched. He was trying to remove a small bell installed on the sliding door, the type that rang when the door was pulled open. As he moved his hand, the bell made a tiny sound. It was too old to install on another house; besides, sliding doors were rarely used in newer houses. He was taking it as a memento, I thought. A small bell that used to ring whenever people came in and out of his house seemed an appropriate item to remember old times with.

But Mr. Hori was there again the next day. In fact, he returned every day, people told me, removing old calendars from the walls and taking out light bulbs. People sensed something was a bit wrong but let it go, thinking he intended to use those things again. Then he started removing glass sliding doors and shōji screens, even tatami mats, which he piled up in the back yard. Each time I passed by the house, the pile of items was larger and higher, until some things were hard to identify. One day I saw him by the faucet facing the street. He was scrubbing a pale green toilet bowl with a brush. I thought then that although Mr. Hori's daughter had a new house, she might be remodeling part of it by using old material. Whoever knew how to get in touch with her must have had the same idea, because no one bothered to tell her about the old man's behavior.

One day a truck drove up. Directed by Mr. Hori, two men in grey uniforms hauled away the tatami mats, the glass doors and the rest of the items. Michi and I watched the truck leave. The consensus among the neighbors was that after all these years Mr. Hori had taken the final step in taking care of his house. Two days later, however, Mr. Hori's daughter and his grandson appeared. After examining the house, the daughter asked a few neighbors what her father had been doing during the past several weeks. Since no one was at her house during the day, the family hadn't even known that the old man had been away. They were naturally astonished when one day they saw all those things piled up in their small yard. When they had asked him what he intended to do with the junk, he wouldn't say anything. He simply stared at the pile, causing his family some alarm.

After this Mr. Hori didn't appear in the neighborhood again.

Soon, other people who had lived at the end of the street moved out one after another. In ordinary situations, people will take their furniture and clean their houses when they leave, but these people, knowing the land developer would sooner or later demolish the entire area, and having been given a great deal of money to move to their new homes, simply didn't bother. They left old furniture in their houses, piles of discarded items in their yards. An old comforter left by the owner of the quilt shop was battered by rain and rapidly faded. The street was littered with old comic books and racing tickets, and every morning I would find some trash in front of our house even though I'd swept the night before. Sweeping again, I would begin to feel the trash was alive and attracted to the light; all of it seemed to come to our house.

Between the well-lit high-rise buildings on one end and the row of stores along the highway on the other, the section in which we lived now formed a sparsely lit valley. Kōta and his friends had fun playing in some of the empty houses but Michi, who was then three years old, was adversely affected by the change. She often started crying in the middle of the night, frightened by something. Seeing this, Father finally decided to move. Summoning Kayoko and her husband one day, he said, "I want you to decide what conditions we'll settle for, and the distribution of the compensation will have to be agreed upon between the four of you. As for me, I'd like to live with my grandchildren as we do now." Then he turned to me and asked, "Is that all right with you, Mieko?" Father always had a certain fortitude within him, while appearing gentle and polite on the surface. Now he seemed to have lost his strength mentally and physically. I sensed it, for example, when I rubbed his legs. Unlike Yūji's, his muscles no longer had flexibility. "That's fine with me, Father," I said.

"Yūji," he then said, addressing his son, "you decide where we're going to move after talking to your mother, Mieko, and the children."

"What is your wish, dear?" asked Mother, and he responded, "To see everyone's wish realized, what else?"

I learned that we would get a large sum of money; it was an amount I'd never dreamed of seeing in my entire life. I was terrified. We decided to use it to pay off Kayoko and Hiroshi's loan, to buy land and a house for us, and the rest would be Father's.

We started to look into the land Hiroshi and Mr. Sawada had recommended. My conditions were that it be convenient for Yūji to commute to work, that it be an environment where

Mother could feel comfortable and where the children could play safely. I said I'd always wanted to live near the sea. Although I felt strongly about the conditions for my husband and children, I didn't consider Father. I thought it would satisfy him if all of us were happy. It was only much later that I realized the newly developed suburb was good for the children but it had no pachinko parlor for Father to walk to.

People in the neighborhood talked about various family problems that had grown obvious since the issue of the land sale was presented to them. It was as if the things that were hidden while families were in a structure called a house suddenly became visible when they had to leave it.

Mr. Gotō had obtained the right to open a cafe in the hotel building. He seemed to be proud of himself when he told us about it, but I sensed the precariousness of his new venture. He, who had been a company employee for many years, was not professional enough even in my eyes to pursue a successful cafe business. He was knowledgeable about coffee and the coffee he made was good, but there was a haughtiness in his attitude, as if he were someone grander than the owner of a cafe. He and his wife moved to a condominium they had rented within walking distance of the hotel. They said they'd spend their compensation on their business since they could buy a house anytime if the business went well. He told us enthusiastically that he'd spend his time learning more about running a cafe until the hotel opened.

The famous jurist still lived with his daughter and granddaughter, Misao, in the Western-style house. When I came to this town, Misao's father had already left, and when her grandfather died I helped with the cooking for the funeral. After finishing two years of college with a major in music, she was now at home, so I asked her to teach Kōta piano once a week. Misao's mother, who rarely left her house, was extremely shy and gave the impression that she had grown older without changing over the years.

Misao invited me to go out with her right before she moved, and one night we went to the other side of the train station to have a drink. Since my marriage, I had rarely gone out at night. There were many more stores using glass in their decor than I had remembered, and the street was much lighter. It seemed to be filled with young people, which probably indicated that I'd grown older. I wondered if I didn't know the town Shinjuku while I lived in the middle of it. Perhaps this section with its glass storefronts is merely its façade while the section I live in is the real Shinjuku, I said to myself. Misao took me to a place with high tables and stools, where loud jazz music was playing. We drank beer.

"I'm quite happy leaving that house. It always smelled musty," Misao said. She must have been twenty-six or seven then, but to me she looked the same as she had when she was in college.

"We're actually saved," she continued. "We were about to face bankruptcy, you see. Mother has never worked and I'm only teaching piano. How do you think we've been supporting ourselves? We're still receiving child support from my father. Can you believe that? Until now Mother and I haven't been able to support ourselves. We needed his money."

"You've got a degree and can play piano. You could've done many things to support yourself," I said, thinking how old-fashioned Misao and her mother seemed.

"Mother didn't want me to work. I couldn't, either. And I think it was because we lived in that house," Misao replied. I wondered what she really meant, and told her my impression of her family.

"Your family has lived in that house since prewar times and so you're different from those who came drifting in after. You're a part of the intellectual class who won't toil for mere money. Is that it?" I asked her.

"I'm not sure. But there's something else. If I get out of that house and live in a condominium where no one knows me, things will be quite different. I know it. To tell you the truth, it's been depressing to be with my mother all the time. I don't know if I can live with her in a new place. This is another reason I feel some change will follow our move."

"My mother's really stubborn," I said to Misao. I felt I could tell her things that I wouldn't tell my husband's family. "My father was a teacher and he came back sick from the war. He died when I was nine years old. My mother taught until last year, although she only substituted during the past few years. She retired last year and decided to enter a nursing home at the foot of Mt. Fuji. There are many retired teachers there and she paid the fee from her retirement money. The Tamiyas had this problem with their land, and so she did this to show she could take care of herself without asking for anyone's help. She didn't say so but I know she was telling me to concern myself only with the Tamiyas. But when she started talking about donating her body after her death, I found it a bit extreme. If you're a donor, she tells me, they'll arrange the funeral and everything else."

Another neighbor, the old woman who ran the dry goods and cigarette shop by herself after her husband died, told us, "I don't know about getting this much money now. But I've already made up my mind. I'll have the welfare people find a nursing home for me when I get too old to move about. That's what I'm going to do. I can use the money to fix our graves, I suppose, but I don't want to buy a condominium. I'm not going to live much longer. I should save the rest to pay for the help I'll need when I become bedridden," she added. When my mother-in-law reminded her that the local government would pay for that, she responded: "Well, I'm sure they'll let you pay while you can." She moved to an apartment not far from where she had lived for many years. "I want you two to take care of my funeral," the old woman used to tell my mother-in-law and me half-jokingly. She was no longer our next-door neighbor.

Our neighbors moved out one by one. Only two houses, ours and the scrap dealer's, were left. Besides these two houses, there was one more house without light or gas service, where a squatter came to live. When more than half of the houses were vacated, the neighborhood filled with a heavy, desolate mood, but when the signs of living were almost completely gone, the mood became peculiarly light. Occasionally I smelled sweet daphne drifting from somewhere.

On the day of our move my father-in-law came upstairs, something he rarely did, and stood on the rooftop deck. From there, on a clear day, one can see Mt. Fuji above the houses and buildings, but on that day it was cloudy. Yūji and I were doing some last minute packing, stuffing a few boxes with children's pajamas and other things, while at the same time trying to calm Kōta down. Moving during school's summer break made him worry and he asked about homework he wouldn't be able to turn in in the fall.

"I'm truly sorry that you two have had to attend to so much of this," said Father, coming into the room and sitting square on the tatami floor. "You must feel regret about leaving."

Yūji and I stopped what we were doing and sat directly facing him. Kōta, his school bag on his lap, watched both his father and grandfather carefully.

Turning down the narrow street from the highway, I looked the other way to see if Kōta might be coming. It was nearly three o'clock. I started walking faster as I approached the greengrocer. I couldn't help feeling guilty that they hadn't received any money from the land development while we, only one street away, had. I hoped they wouldn't see me.

"Oh hi, Mrs. Tamiya," the greengrocer's wife called out. "You're here to try out the hotel today?" she asked. "My, you've gotten big, Micchan," she added, smiling broadly.

"Things have changed so much around here I can't tell what's what. But now standing in front of your store like this, I remember," I said.

Some bushes had been planted where our house had stood. I looked up at the face of the twenty-story white rectangular hotel. It reminded me of a gigantic pack of cigarettes. It was hard to tell the depth of the building from such an angle.

"You should stop by Mr. Gotō's cafe," the greengrocer's wife said. "I told Misao, too."

"Is Misao here, then?"

"Everybody came by here today. Trying to get to the hotel from the other direction was too confusing, they told me. I saw a red foreign car go that way," she said, pointing in the direction where the car scrapping plant had been.

"Was the young Mrs. wearing her mink and diamond?" I asked.

"I didn't see any mink or diamond," the greengrocer's wife replied.

She didn't seem to be as concerned about this land business as I had feared. Is she happy just being healthy and able to work every day? I wondered. She certainly seemed that way, but there's no way to tell for sure. I'd learned that people were often not as they seemed. I bought three boxes of strawberries and asked about her mother-in-law.

"She's fine. But I'm sorry to hear about your father," she said.

She knew about it then. I wondered if she considered his death Yūji's and my fault.

"Say hello to your grandma from me," she said to Michi, handing her a bag of strawberries.

We walked to the front entrance of the hotel and went down the escalator two floors to the basement, to Mr. Gotō's cafe. It smelled of paint and freshly cut wood. Some interior work was still being done inside restaurants that already had their signs up. There were two cafes on that floor. As I pushed one of the doors open I heard Mr. Gotō's voice greeting us from the other side of the counter. Misao, sitting on the stool, turned around and saw us. "Hi, Micchan," she cried out. "Would you like to sit here, please?" Mr. Gotō pointed to the seat next to Misao. I sensed some change in him, and it wasn't only because he was wearing a black vest and ribbon tie instead of the ordinary clothes he used to wear.

"Mother and I aren't getting along well," Misao said when Mr. Gotō had left after taking our order. "Did you make a lot of friends, Micchan?" she then asked Michi, who extended her hand in response and folded her fingers.

"Not getting along?" I asked Misao.

"About a year and half after we moved to the condominium I decided I didn't want to live with her anymore. It's my own problem, but I just felt I didn't want to talk to her, sometimes I didn't even want to go home. So I rented an apartment and left."

"Did you find someone you want to be with?" I asked. She shook her head.

"Mother asked the same question. It wasn't anything like that. I just wanted to live alone. I told her I'd visit her once in a while, but Mother took it wrong and she left the condominium, too. So there's no one living there now. Isn't that a bit strange?"

Mr. Gotō brought coffee for me and orange juice for Michi, then left quietly without a word and disappeared to the back of the counter.

"And how is your mother doing now?"

"She's in a small cheap apartment," Misao replied. "As if she's competing with me. We divided the money left over after we bought the condominium, and so I've got enough. It's strange, but now that I have my own money, I don't feel like spending it on myself. I'm working now. I'm a nursery school teacher. I think Mother felt the same way I did. She couldn't change as easily, but it seems she's trying to become more independent."

What did money mean to Misao and her mother, I wondered. Whatever it was, it certainly had a strange effect on them.

"I invited her today and reserved two rooms in case she didn't want to share the same room. She hasn't come yet but I'm glad I invited her."

I thought of my own mother who was now in a nursing home. I didn't invite her since I knew she'd decline. But I should have invited her anyway, I thought. We should feel free to ask more of each other.

"I hope your mother will come," I said to Misao.

"Where's Kōta?" she asked Michi.

"He's riding his bicycle from Yokohama. He should be here now. Why don't you come and see him? We're in room 1801," I told Misao.

Mr. Gotō didn't talk to us and said nothing about himself. Three other customers were there, along with a waiter and a cashier. I wondered if Mr. Gotō was trying to imply in his detached manner that the old relationship of landowner and tenant no longer existed between us.

Entering room 1801, I looked for Kōta among the people there. I saw Kayoko and her husband, but not Kōta. "Where's Kōta?" I asked, before apologizing for taking so long to do the shopping.

"He called a few minutes ago. He's more than an hour and a half behind schedule. He won't be here before five."

"Masaru said he should've ridden his bike, too," Kayoko said. "He's making a tour of the hotel with Grandma now."

"How did Mother like the room?" I asked Yūji. I shouldn't have asked this in front of Hiroshi but I wondered if she liked the way its interior was done.

Yūji, like his father, was small-boned while Hiroshi had a large build and a quiet manner. They sat on the floor, relaxed and drinking their whiskey.

The room's black interior had been agreed upon between Yūji and Hiroshi before Father died. They thought of changing it afterward; Yūji even considered abandoning the idea of keeping this room. He thought perhaps it would be better to forget the old town entirely.

"This is fine. The way we'd planned it when Dad was still

alive is fine," Yūji said as if he was talking to himself.

"Yes, I think so, too," said Kayoko. "When Masaru said earlier that next time he'd come here riding his bike, I realized we'd done the right thing by keeping this room for ourselves."

I heard a knocking at the door and opened it, hoping it was Kōta. It was Mr. Sawada of the land development company.

"I'm really sorry about your father . . ." he said. Kayoko, who had heard the voice from the next room, craned her neck. "Ah, Mr. Sawada, please come in," she said. It's rare for Kayoko to be friendly like this to people she doesn't know well. Yūji and Hiroshi also invited him in.

Mr. Sawada took his shoes off and sat on the floor near the entryway, repeating his words of condolence as he bowed deeply.

"Come this way, please," I told him, inviting him to sit at the table. Then I stood up to wash the strawberries.

"We've had such trouble with the folks at the car scrapping place," said Mr. Sawada, smiling wryly. "We've arranged rooms today so that the brothers won't see each other. I wish all the families I had to deal with were like you Tamiyas."

"Where should I wash these?" I wondered aloud holding the strawberries in my hand. "I don't feel like using the bathroom sink."

"That'll be all right. Here, I'll wash," said Kayoko, taking the strawberry boxes from me.

"We've just been talking about that. Hotels have many conveniences but they're not so great as living spaces," said Hiroshi as he put ice in a glass and poured whiskey into it for Mr. Sawada.

"I'm sorry the stores on the basement floors haven't all

opened yet," he said as if he represented the hotel. He declined the whiskey.

"I've been thinking about this for a long time, Mr. Sawada," said Kayoko from the bathroom. "So tell me, who decides to build a bunch of high rises around here, or, for that matter, in any other place? Where are those decisions made? They certainly seem to be made while people who live there know nothing about them. I just don't understand."

"I wondered about that, too," I said, while thinking that there was no sense in asking Mr. Sawada. "Who benefits from all this in the end?"

Mr. Sawada was silent and kept his head bowed.

"But the issue is beyond us individuals," Hiroshi said. "It's at a higher level, like the talk of making Tokyo a truly international city before Hong Kong's ninety-nine-year lease expires."

"I heard this the other day from one of my colleagues," Yūji said as if he were trying to appease Kayoko. "His wife's mother had a house in Daikanyama, which she rented out to a foreign family since it cost her too much to keep up and pay the taxes. She'd had a small house built for herself at the corner of the lot. My collegue's wife had been unhappy that her family had ended up like that, but while visiting his grandmother his teenage son became good friends with the tenant. My colleague says it's probably just the older generation and us who are hung up with extended families, hometowns and things like that."

"I still want to hear the response that would satisfy people in situations similar to my father's," Kayoko repeated. Mr. Sawada, who had been looking down until then, suddenly stood up and walked toward the bathroom. All of us watched him in surprise.

"I've wanted to have a good talk for once with a person like you," he said in a different, rougher tone of voice, slouching against the wall by the entrance to the bathroom. "Because I agree with what you say."

"What do you mean?" Kayoko's voice trembled. Hiroshi stood up.

"You asked a good question. I want to take you to see where I'm from," continued Mr. Sawada. As Hiroshi was about to walk toward him, Mr. Sawada suddenly bowed once again and said: "Well, thank you very much." He put on his shoes deliberately and left. We stood there not knowing what had happened. Something had happened, though, that was clear. Michi, sitting on the sofa, swung her legs back and forth. Kayoko came out of the bathroom with the strawberries, her entire body shaking. She burst into tears. I understood both Kayoko's feelings and Mr. Sawada's attitude. I felt like throwing down the glass in my hand and having a good cry too.

"I wonder where my home is," said Hiroshi. Kayoko was sobbing now. She went to the bathroom and washed her face and when she came back she looked somewhat refreshed. Was that Mr. Sawada's last job then, I wondered, feeling a bit strange.

"Hasn't Kōta arrived yet?" asked Mother after a while.

"Don't worry," said Hiroshi. "I talked to him on the phone awhile ago; he sounded like he was doing fine."

"The children here are getting hungry. We should start now," suggested Yūji.

"No, we should wait," Masaru said.

"Let's have a toast then," I said, suggesting that we toast again when Kōta arrived. I poured whiskey into three glasses, including one for Father, beer for us three women and Coca-cola for the children. I placed a glass on the table and we all toasted.

"Quite a lot of people are here today, aren't there?" said Mother. She must have seen the families I'd seen earlier down in the lobby; perhaps it was sinking in that this was now a public place where anyone could come whenever they wanted.

The sky was changing from pale to dark blue. The windows of the high-rise buildings might be lit up now but all we could see from our windows were clusters of red and yellow lights along the streets. They weren't very clear yet, fading into the grey landscape of the town.

When the telephone rang, I thought it was Kōta. "Is that you, Kōta?" I said and Masaru and Michi looked at me expectantly.

"Oh, hi. This is Misao. Is Kōta not there yet?" It was Misao calling to say that she couldn't come to visit us. Her mother had arrived, she said. She sounded close to tears.

"So your mother's come. I'm glad she did," I said.

I explained to Mother that we'd met Misao at Mr. Gotō's cafe.

"I hope Kōta isn't in trouble," said Masaru. "If I had my bike here, I could go and meet him." The idea that Father wasn't the only one missing at this family gathering somehow made the adults feel less anxious. Michi stood by the window watching the lights outside, which had become brighter.

"It's getting quite dark," someone said.

"I wonder if I could spot the bicycle's headlight," said Masaru. Everybody was quiet after that, waiting for the telephone to ring. At six o'clock there was still no phone call.

"I'm worried about Kōta," said Mother, and at that moment the phone rang. It was Kōta. He was nearly in tears.

"Give it to me," Yūji said, grabbing the phone from me. "Kōta, tell me where you are," he said gently. "Tell me what you see around you. You have lots of ten-yen coins, don't you? Put two more in now so you won't get disconnected." He turned toward us to tell us that Kōta seemed to be lost somewhere among the high-rise buildings. Kōta couldn't describe any of the nearby buildings. I remembered how I'd felt when I looked up at the hotel from outside its entryway. It would be quite difficult to tell where you were inside the cluster of high rises. Besides, Kōta had never walked around this town at night.

"If we look out from the window of the other room, we could tell the shapes of various buildings in the distance," said Masaru.

"That's true," Yūji said to Masaru, and turned to the phone again. "Listen, Kōta," he said slowly. "We've got a good idea. You'll be fine. You've got the phone number of this hotel, right? You dial that number and ask to be connected to room 1851. You've got that? That's right. Then Dad and Masaru will direct you from the window. We can tell where you are from there. Don't worry, we can do it. You hang up now and call again."

Yūji and Masaru rushed out of the room. Following them, Michi, Kayoko and I all ran into the room across the corridor. In room 1851 Yūji took the phone toward the window and waited. When it rang, he immediately picked it up. "Yes, go ahead please," he said. "Look around you now," he said slowly to his son, "and tell me what shape of building you can see. What? A spaceship? The Yamato?" He sounded perplexed.

"I don't think you understand," Masaru said. "Let me

try." Masaru took the phone and faced the window. "Hello, Kōta, this is Masaru. I'll guide you out of there now, okay? I'm here on the eighteenth floor control room of the Planet Hotel. When you look around, it looks like a lot of space ships floating around in the dark, doesn't it? All right. Now, can you find any other buildings that remind you of anything?"

Masaru listened for awhile. "Something like a ghost stretching its arms," he then said to Michi. Michi gazed outside intently.

"And what can you see behind you?" Masaru asked again. "He says he sees something like a ruler," he then told Michi. "Keep looking in the same direction." Masaru, talking now on the phone, looked outside with Michi. She pointed with her index finger. Masaru followed her direction and nodded.

"Kōta, go ahead and face the direction where you saw that, and put three more coins in. Now, turn your face to where your shoulder is and face that direction. Did you do that? Then you'll see a tall skinny building in front. It should look like a sideways cassette tape case. Yes, we can see that from here also," Masaru went on talking to Kōta.

Masaru then asked for a map, and when I handed him a map of the street around the hotel, he continued to give directions on the phone.

"If you go on that street, curving to the left a little bit, you'll see the building that looks like it's falling on you on your left. You pass that and go on further, and then you'll see the building that looks like a ruler. You wait at the entrance of the building. If you can't find the entrance, just wait anywhere by the building. You understand? You think you can do it? Don't forget to collect the unused coins. If you have to call again, you'll need them. Don't forget your phone number, too. Your dad'll come meet you now. I'll stay in the control room."

"Kōta's coming from over there toward the other side of that building," Masaru said to Yūji when he hung up the phone. "If you find him, call me." Yūji left the room saying that he would go there by taxi although it was quite close by. "It's not so close, is it?" said Michi to Masaru.

Masaru and Michi were looking out the window, and Hiroshi also went to it, gazing out. Various windows were now lit, some far and some near, floating in the darkness. What you saw out there now seemed quite different from what you'd see during the day.

The telephone rang again. Masaru, who answered it, said "Yes," and gave a sign to Michi making a V shape with his fingers. "Roger," he said, putting down the telephone. Kayoko asked her son if we could all go back to the other room.

When we returned to the room with the black interior, we found Mother sitting there alone. We all sat down without a word. By the way he was breathing, I could tell that Marasu hadn't recovered from his excitment. Hiroshi was studying the map.

"Grandma," Masaru said after awhile, "when Grandpa's soul comes back here, it'll get lost, won't it?"

"Don't worry," Mother replied. "Your grandpa's seen lots of things that have changed."

"Does he know that we're here now?"

"He might. He might find you if you close your eyes." said Mother. Masaru and Michi closed their eyes.

"He's there, but not quite," said Michi. I was a bit frightened but Michi looked quite calm, sitting on the sofa and swinging her legs.

"Ah," cried Michi in a low voice. "He's here."

Masaru and Michi opened their eyes and looked toward the door. The rest of us did the same, looking toward the door expectantly.

Straw Dogs

Taeko Tomioka

Eikichi was in the habit of saying "To make it short." I had no idea what he was making short, but he certainly liked the expression.

My favorite question was, "What would you do if we had a baby?" I always asked this question after I'd had sex with a young man, and I always looked forward to hearing their responses. This time Eikichi didn't say "to make it short"; he was silent.

"Well, what would you do? Shall I mail it to you through U.P.S.?" I said, smiling. Eikichi looked relieved. But he still couldn't come up with any response to my teasing. I didn't pursue the question. It was only the initial reaction I found interesting.

More than once Eikichi had said that his name reminded people of an old man's name. He said it was his grandad who had named him. Not "grandfather" nor "grandpa" but "grandad"; that's what he called him. Seventy-some years old now, he was a farmer in the countryside.

Ever since he'd entered the room I'd thought of nothing except what I could do to get Eikichi to have sex with me. No actually, it wasn't only since he'd entered the room, rather I'd been thinking of nothing but seducing him ever since the first time I saw him. This was not just the case with Eikichi. I've always wondered whether a relationship can be established simply by the entry of part of a stranger's body into mine.

Eikichi hadn't said a word since he'd taken off his clothes. Our sex ended quickly. He didn't look embarrassed. He didn't attempt to explain. After he dressed he talked for a while about his dormitory and the people he worked with, frequently using the expression "to make it short." He also talked about a cheap nightclub he went to once with a guy from work.

"To make it short, I'll say that the girls are better off. The popular ones at that club are only twenty-one or so, the same age as I am, and they earn ten times what I make. They can make that much money simply because they're women." He became more adamant about the topic as he went on.

Listening to him, I said to myself: He'll tell his roommate at the dorm about this, our single encounter in our physical "relationship." He'll make it into a funny story. "To make it short, those ladies, those middle-aged women, aren't actually bad at all," he might say. Eikichi hadn't held my hand, and he didn't try to kiss me. When I sat on the bed, he went ahead and took off his clothes as if he were about to take a bath.

I've always been amazed by how easily and quickly that part of the male body can enter the female body. It seems almost comical the way it so smoothly slides inside me, and momentarily appears to achieve physical unity. Although this unity happens quickly and with amazing ease, most people expect connection to continue on through the dramatic stages of conflict, cooperation, ecstasy, and so on. I did not expect any of those dramatic experiences with Eikichi or, for that matter, with any other young men.

Still, each time I find that I'm impressed, even moved, by the fact that this part of a total stranger's body can come inside me so easily. Eikichi, for instance, was a complete stranger until yesterday. Today he is not only here with me, but for a while his body is inside me. I can't help marveling at the fact that a man who'd been walking outside on the boulevard in his suit came into a room and became naked. It was strange to see a naked man standing in front of me wearing only a wrist watch. Once I saw a naked body wearing only socks, which I found amusing. Another time I was struck by the sight of part of a man's penis showing under the hem of a white cotton undershirt. For some reason Eikichi didn't take off his wrist watch when he removed his clothes, and he didn't use that commonplace technique of sliding it off against my skin. I liked him because of this. When he was done, he stood up like a person who'd just finished moving his bowels and he put on his clothes, returning to his original self.

I didn't know why Eikichi had responded to my invitation and why he'd come without asking questions—I didn't care to find out. I only looked forward to the moment when a stranger, more specifically a young man I'd taken a fancy to, would enter my body, slipping inside me. I had no interest in finding out whether he did so because he was curious, or because he wanted to achieve ejaculation, or because he was attracted to me. As a rule I do not see the same man twice. What I couldn't help expecting was that a young man like Eikichi would be left with a certain vile feeling, an awful aftertaste, when the act was over. A woman who was no longer young, a total stranger, had made a pass at him and he had gone to bed with her without the involvement of either money or love. Secretly I expected to see this create a small, inexplicable dark space in his mind. Eikichi didn't satisfy this expectation. But his lack of response gave me a kind of sadistic pleasure.

"Sure, I've been to one of those places before, but the cafes with private booths were something else. With those setups you can't call it a cafe any more. When I used to go to them you could sometimes see a woman's leg sticking out from the bottom of a thin curtain, you know. To make it short, people went there because they didn't have money to go to a hotel, don't you think so?"

Eikichi was chatting away as if he were talking to his buddy. According to him, these cafes had booths lined up in a row, like train compartments, each with two small chairs and a table only big enough to hold two tea cups. They were divided by a thin board. When a man and a woman sit next to each other in these booths, there's no space for them to move about. In these booths young couples kissed and caressed each other, even had intercourse, Eikichi told me. No matter what people said, the space was too small for intercourse, so sometimes the table was kicked over and cups fell and broke. At other times you might hear a male voice trying to suppress a cry of excitement and see a woman's leg flying out through the curtain.

"Guys who have money wouldn't go to such a tacky place. To make it short, it's us who came out of the sticks with ninth-grade educations who would go there. If you're one of those who has his own room and parents who pay the rent, you wouldn't go to such a place. But if you live in a dorm you've got no choice. It's the same with girls most of the time. They agree to come along because they're interested in sex, right? But in the end most of them don't like it there. After letting you touch them a lot they say they won't do it in a place like that. In those days all I thought of was doing it. Thinking about it now, I was miserable, you know. All you'd see was a woman's leg sticking out from under a dirty curtain. You'd hear the noises from the next booth, you'd hear the guy asking to be let in. It's really cramped there, one square meter, that's all. Guys who can take women wherever they want in a car would never understand the feeling. To make it short, it reminds you of the night train carrying groups of kids into the city to work." Eikichi finished talking. Then he drank his tea, apparently without enjoying it, and prepared to go. When he returned to his dormitory, he would tell his roommates about his sexual encounter. As he was leaving, a gold metal button fell off his black sport coat. He picked it up carefully and put it in his pocket.

Yōji Tomoda left the university without graduating from the drama department when he was accepted by a theater group as a student actor. Soon he was given the lead in a play, a small studio production.

I saw Yōji for the first time on the day of the group's initial script reading. The moment I saw him I began fantasizing about having sex with him. He wasn't particularly good-looking but his features were large, well suited to a stage actor. He wore a black sweater and jeans, and carried his script in a dirty canvas bag.

"I saw a large mole on Yō's chest," said the middle-aged actress who played opposite him, smiling.

Yoji Tomoda was called Yō by the people in his theater group, who were all older than he was. When the producer said something to him, he simply said "yes." He wasn't talkative; between rehearsals he rarely spoke unless he had to.

I'd decided to wait until closing night. In the meantime I tried not to speak to him.

"Yōji isn't bad, what do you think?" the producer said to me.

"He's your type," said the actress. I felt that they were

both trying to encourage me. It sounded as though the producer was asking my opinion of Yōji as a young man rather than as an actor.

"Yō, come and sit next to this lady," the actresses would say, pointing at me whenever we sat down to eat between rehearsals. Since no one in the group was his age, Yōji was isolated most of the time.

However, once he started acting, Yōji's voice was loud and powerful. He wasn't intimidated by the two middle-aged, experienced actresses. This attitude didn't seem to stem from naiveté; rather he seemed to be challenging someone, though not specifically the actress who played across from him. He was possessed by a free-floating, inexplicable anger.

"Yō's something else. During the second scene when he pushes me against the wall, trying to embrace me, you know, he kept stroking my back with his left hand. He knew no one could see it," said one of the actresses, the shorter one. They all laughed a little.

"Maybe there's a stage direction in his script," said the other actress. She seemed to have something in mind. They all laughed again. Yōji, who'd heard them as he came in carrying tea for everyone, didn't laugh.

"Do men serve tea here?" I asked.

"Yō is a student actor, not yet a member, that's why," said one of the actresses.

Rehearsals are usually boring for those who aren't involved in the play, but I went to the studio frequently in order to see Yōji. During my visits I didn't speak to him at all.

The two actresses are about the same age as I am, and I've known the tall one for many years. She is a large woman, but she has a voice and manner of speech too dainty for her role. However, when I heard her speak to Yōji her voice sounded cruel. I empathized with Yōji and felt his humiliation.

The closing night party wasn't very big. After all, it had only been a studio performance with three players. We went to a bar nearby and had some beer and snacks. Still, there ended up being about twenty of us altogether, including stage hands, friends of the players and a few other members of the group. Yōji, who had served tea during rehearsals, refrained from serving drinks at the bar. He sat alone in the corner with his beer.

"I know you were looking at Yō all the time, I was watching you from on stage. It's disgusting," said the tall actress. She repeated this many times.

"I think Tomoda played well," said the producer, calling Yōji by his surname, with a hint of formality in his voice.

"Yō, come here now. The main actor can't be sitting in a corner," someone said, inviting him to join the producer and the actresses. He came, glass in hand, and sat diagonally across from me. After a while the stage hands and the producer left. Only a few of us remained in the bar.

"Please excuse me now. I have a rehearsal tomorrow," said Yōji to the actresses.

"You're in the next one, too?"

"Yes. A soldier," said Yōji. Soldiers simply walk across the stage when they aren't standing, so this meant he was returning to his original status of student actor.

The actresses and their friends started talking about Yōji, making it difficult for him to leave. Again they brought up the fact that I had been looking at him on stage.

"Mr. Tomoda, why don't we go somewhere else to drink?" I said, keeping my eyes on him as I stood up.

The others were amazed at my brazenness and watched us leave without a word.

Outside the bar there was a narrow street with cars lined up on one side. It was a place where taxis often waited for fares. When I realized I'd been grabbing Yōji's upper arm, I let it go and held his hand instead.

"We were able to get rid of those middle-aged women, weren't we?" I said. This was the first time I'd spoken since we'd left the bar.

"Let's go get a drink somewhere," said Yōji in a tone quite different from that I'd heard at rehearsals; he sounded like a young man talking to a friend.

He soon went back, however, to being reticent, even gloomy. It was rather cold out, but instead of a coat he wore a thin black sweater and pale blue jeans. He had on white high-top shoes, and carried his dirty canvas shoulder bag. He could pass as a student, but perhaps not as an actor. While we walked I kept telling myself that I had to make love to this man, as if I were on an important mission. I heard the loud voices of the actresses and the others talking all at once inside my head. You guys don't have to fuss and talk so loud, I answered them silently, with peculiar confidence. I won't fail to carry this out.

Yōji didn't attempt to pull his hand away from mine, and he didn't say anything. Earlier he had said that he wanted to drink more, but now he kept walking. He looked as glum as a student who'd just failed his entrance exams.

"Was it nice after that?" the tall actress would ask a few days afterward.

"I'm not interested in kiddy menus," I would say, to put a stop to her curiosity.

But now I started to feel depressed with Yōji next to me.

When I realized that walking with his hand firmly in mine meant that we already had a physical relationship, I felt as if my sweaty hand were a part of my sex organs. I released his hand.

"Do you want to play pachinko?" Yōji asked when we came to a big pinball game parlor. Loud music blasted from inside. I told him I disliked pachinko. However, I couldn't think of a bar I could take Yōji to, and I disliked being with people who drank anyway. What I wanted was to find some place, like a shady spot under a tree, where we could sniff each other's bodies as animals do. Cafes with private booths like the one Eikichi described might exist for such purposes, but I couldn't imagine going to one of them, it wasn't my style. Now I didn't know what to do with my fussiness.

I kept walking, holding Yōji's arm. I sensed in him the humiliation and anger of a youth who, though first mentioning more drinking, had ended up inviting me to play pachinko. I felt like pouncing on his shame as if it were some helpless prey. Yōji wasn't glum just because a woman had made a pass at him, or because he was broke, or, for that matter, because he lacked the smooth words to turn the situation around. There was something else. I wanted to pull out the guts of his dark mood and devour them with my teeth. This desire was combined with my strange sense that my mission was to make love to him. I wondered if Yōji was humiliated because he sensed that he was being insulted by a woman. Perhaps his embarrassment was made all the more real because there hadn't been any sex between us. I continued to walk with Yōji, holding onto his arm. I must not do anything until he makes a move, I said to myself.

Before sex with Eikichi, I had fed him steak. Blood scattered from the steak as it cooked in the frying pan. When the blood mixed with fat, it turned transparent as water and ran out from the meat. This is like feeding and fattening an animal before slaughter, I'd thought as I watched Eikichi enjoying the food I offered. Now I wanted this gloomy Yōji to do something entirely different, but I was too anxious to wait until his shame and anger were neatly wrapped up, like tempura in batter, fried, and ready to eat.

We came across a takoyaki snack wagon. I bought a plateful and ate some as I walked. Yōji walked a few steps ahead of me, and when I offered him the takoyaki, he pretended not to hear. I thought if I had been a friend or a sweetheart his own age, he would eat. Or, perhaps if he didn't want to eat while walking, he would have said something like, "Don't do that; it's unsightly."

"But it's really good. People tease me for liking them so much, but these are my favorite snack. I can't resist the smell," I told Yōji in a loud voice. He walked ahead of me, looking even more despondent. However, he didn't leave me.

"Wait, don't walk so fast. My right leg's stiff. I have neuralgia, and when I get chilled, it gets worse," I said to Yōji. Then I grabbed his arm, dragging my leg. The neuralgia bit was only partly true. It was a ploy I used frequently to jar young men with the fact that they were going to have sex with an older woman.

I saw a telephone booth and went inside to check the yellow pages. Watching Yōji standing outside the booth, I dialed the numbers of several hotels, none of which had vacancies. I was finally able to make reservations at the last hotel, the furthest out and the most expensive. I stopped a taxi and told the driver to take us there. When we got to the hotel, I paid for the room. Then I tapped Yōji on the shoulder with the plastic tag which the room key was fastened to, and made him follow me.

He'd been standing in front of the elevator like an animal that had been drenched in rain. Don't make an issue of your shame or anger now; you came with me because you wanted to, I said silently while we were in the elevator. I looked at him as if he were already my lover. There is really nothing two strangers, a male and a female, can do but have sex.

Yōji didn't undress as if he were about to take a bath, like Eikichi had done. He remained silent except when he pulled open the curtain and said how beautiful the lighted streets were. When I turned around, there was this man in brand new, white underpants instead of a black sweater and soiled jeans. For a fleeting moment the whiteness of his underpants told me something about his life. Then he slid under the white sheet without taking them off and lay there with his head sticking out.

"I've never been in an expensive hotel like this," he said distantly.

While I'd been walking with Yōji, I'd spotted places beneath trees where an animal straying from its herd could take refuge and rest. I thought such a place would make this young man feel more comfortable and natural. We were not like those rutting young lovers who went to cafes with private booths and let their legs stick out from the curtains. What we actually did, however, was the same. It was obvious that Yōji disliked this "expensive hotel," but I was ready to attack his gloom. Never mind his mood, I said to myself, trying to suppress a cruelty inside me.

His young, slender torso covered mine, and before I knew it, that part of him slipped into me. Somehow, from that moment on, I began to feel how superb Yōji's body was. It wasn't because of his sexual experience; it was something more subtle, as if his body actively sought physical contact with other bodies. This was a quality I'm sure he was born with. I remembered how this tongue-tied, gloomy youth had talked on stage in such a strong, sure voice. I felt at this moment that he was still on stage. His whole body seemed to reach every corner of mine. And yet I didn't think he was acting. There was an innate expressiveness to his body. He wasn't experienced with women and he didn't try to conceal it, nor did he take his partner for granted. His body told all of this eloquently. I was moved by this.

"You've done something naughty to Yō," said the tall actress to me sometime later.

"I didn't do anything naughty. I did something good," I replied.

Women my age are interested in the details of sex. They are eager to hear about the stage setting and dialogue which surrounded the act, and the techniques the male partner used to induce physical delight. I wasn't interested in giving out any details, and the actress' curiosity remained unsatisfied.

"A good thing? Was it very good?" she kept asking.

"Yes, it was good, so good that I contemplated a double suicide."

"How frightful! But I'm relieved. I thought you had some problem in that area. People tell me you're seducing young men right and left."

"Thanks for your concern but I think I'm normal. I believe in getting what I need, no more. I don't expect more than I need. But what I did with Mr. Tomoda was beyond my needs, you see."

"Then you're fickle."

"If you call it fickle, life itself is fickle."

"You're disgusting, as always."

Yōji spoke little and responded with his body to what I, a stranger, sought from him, and I understood intuitively what type of person he was. He approached me as an equal. His body was not affected by my age or my social status. I sensed some hostility, but he didn't seem to be conscious of it. His withdrawn mood continued and it excited me. By the bed I saw a pair of neatly placed white shoes. Yōji Tomoda told me he was twenty-two years old.

I was surprised that he was still next to me when I woke up around six the next morning. Without opening his eyes he thrust his knee between my legs, and instantly his body was united with mine. In a moment of confusion, I thought we were lovers. He used his body as if he knew me well, and I couldn't help noticing his tendency toward a kind of commonplace male sincerity. I was slightly disappointed. I also felt peaceful, and lay there awhile.

I left the hotel alone. Stepping outside, I was assaulted by the bright light of morning and the sight of people on their way to work. The sight hit me like hard rain on concrete. In spite of such an assault, I did not let myself fall to the ground.

Shunsuke seemed to enjoy talking to me, but he gave no hint that he had sexual interest in women. His body didn't give off the semen smell characteristic of most young men. His thin chest, skinny loins and childish face made him look like a high school student. But he said he was twenty-four years old. He was the nephew of a friend, and he'd been sent to my house by his uncle. When I met him, as usual I thought only of sex. I wouldn't have been interested if he had been one of those young men who seem to have semen stuck to their skin.

"You wear interesting clothes," I said, running my hand down the back of his jacket to the jeans that tightly covered his waist and loins. His jacket had a down lining, the kind that people wear for outdoor sports. It was bright red.

"You're warm from the waist up, but you must be cold down here. Tight jeans don't have any space for air, you know. Down is warm because it allows for a lot of air," I said.

"I heard ostrich down is hard to come by nowadays so they use guinea hens. But I think this is ostrich," Shunsuke said, smiling.

"When I'm on the train and a boy like you wearing tight jeans comes and stands in front of me, I always stare at him, you know. I wonder how that thing in there is doing in those tight jeans."

Shunsuke laughed in a childish way.

"Would you mind having a date with me next Sunday?" I said. I held his hand as he laughed innocently.

"Sure, it's okay." He looked at me expectantly.

"Then kiss me to show you've promised."

Shunsuke clumsily held my head between his hands, and I touched his chest. I felt the thumping of his heart; it made me think of ejaculation, not the pulsing of blood.

"Don't tell your uncle," I said, making him my accomplice.

The following Sunday, when I spotted him standing by the ticket booth, I was disappointed. Although I didn't expect him to come in a three-piece suit, I'd hoped to see him dressed in something other than such ordinary clothes. There was nothing about his dress or manner to indicate he was taking an overnight trip with a woman. He wore his usual jeans, an ordinary shirt and jacket, and carried a leather shoulder bag which he seemed to have with him all the time. He was tall and skinny, and looked like a teenager. But he'd arranged for train tickets, a hotel reservation and an itinerary without a hitch. And before he boarded the train he bought all the necessities: a newspaper, a magazine, cigarettes, canned beer, some peanuts, chocolates and Kleenex.

At the hotel, which was the oldest and best known in the area, Shunsuke inquired about departure times for the cable car and the pleasure boat. When we got to our room he immediately turned on the shower to check the water pressure. "This building was built in the old days," he commented.

"The boat leaves at four. We can make it if we go now," he said after a while.

"Let's do it tomorrow," I said, moving close to him.

The room was bright with strong sunlight leaking through the shutter of the western window. I was interested in nothing but sex with this man who looked like a high school student. I wanted to find out if sex would make some kind of connection between us.

Shunsuke started to take off his clothes and asked if I wanted him to undress. Then he placed his jeans, shirt and underwear neatly on the back of a chair; even his socks were paired together. My clothes were scattered here and there on the floor.

"What would you do if we had a baby?"

"I'd put it on my back and go to school with a milk bottle," he said.

Through sex I try to discover something metaphysical

about my and my partner's body. This is why I allow my body to be completely exposed, like a bag being turned inside out, with my sex organ as the opening. I'm curious to know if there are such things as spirituality and maliciousness hidden in the corners of this bag, waiting to be revealed when the bag is turned inside out by a stranger's sex organ. Shunsuke lifted one of my legs, and I wondered what he saw in there. "Is this good?" he asked, and I said, "More." "Look more carefully," was what I meant to say. The fluid coming out of my body would instantly dry up if my body were turned inside out.

The naked body of a man stepped across the stripes of sunlight made by the blinds. There was no trace of the darkness I'd felt moments ago as I clung to this thin, naked body; it had disappeared the way mist blows away. I felt comfortable, as if I'd just had a bath. Touching the shoulders of strangers always alarms me when I walk in crowded places; my body tenses. People's gazes often make me feel so uncomfortable that I look away. And yet I held the naked body of this man, a stranger, simply because I felt like it. This woman, who is reluctant even to shake hands with people when such a formality is required, connected her body to a stranger's without hesitation. This is a mystery, I thought, while absently gazing at Shunsuke's naked back in the stripes of sunlight. He had none of the heavy sullenness that I'd seen in Yōji.

"I find it erotic to do this at this time of the day, don't you?" said Shunsuke.

"What? Erotic? Why?"

The word "erotic" repulsed me; it stuck in my throat. And I'd lost interest in him now that sex was over.

A man's small buttock was in front of my eyes, looking like

an alien thing. Now it was on the other side of a plastic shower curtain, with hot water splashing over it. I sat on the toilet seat. The wet face of a stranger peered from the plastic curtain. Shocked to find a woman on the toilet, he disappeared back inside.

"It's all right, you can come out. Haven't you ever seen a woman peeing before? You can see it now," I said to him. The stranger rushed out of the bathroom, all wet, trying not to see the woman. Inside the toilet bowl I noticed some opaque fluid floating. The semen of this man-boy. Suddenly, I felt like laughing—the whole thing seemed comical. There must be men who have wives at age twenty-four, some even have children. Shunsuke came here with me like a boy being invited to a picnic. He showed he knew how to deal with a woman in bed. He wasn't even timid when he caressed me. Afterward, he took a shower, enjoying it like a child would after a play in the pool.

"We should have our dinner somewhere else. I heard there are some well-known restaurants here that serve freshwater fish," said the man-boy in tight jeans, cheerfully.

I opened the blinds and I saw a lake in the distance. I felt like staying in the room, alone.

"Doesn't this view of the lake make you want to try double suicide?" I said. I wanted to provoke him. Sightseeing wasn't what I had in mind at all. Shunsuke looked at me, bewildered. His slender torso and long, skinny legs were now in his clothes; his white-socked feet inside his high-top shoes. When he talked, his canine teeth showed a bit. I thought a lover might find this charming.

"Don't you feel like going somewhere now, just disappearing?"

"Shall we? Let's go somewhere far away," he said. He called me by name for the first time. Then he looked down with an intensity in his face, provoked by my words. I felt that my interest in him would last another day.

"Does your mother wear glasses?" I asked Shunsuke later as I took my glasses out to read the menu. This was one of my usual schemes, like my neuralgia bit, although I actually did need glasses.

"I think she uses them when she reads."

"I can't read anything without my glasses, even if I go like this," I said, holding the menu away from me.

"Have you had that problem since you were a child?"

"Don't be silly. These are bifocals."

Shunsuke just looked at me, not knowing what to say.

"There's nothing strange about wearing these after forty, you know."

"But you don't look so. . . ."

"Appearance and reality are two different things," I said, staring at Shunsuke's face through my glasses.

"I don't believe you're forty," he said in an angry voice.

"But I am."

"Still, I do want to go somewhere far and disappear," I added after a while.

"You don't mean abroad, do you? I know I can manage anywhere in Japan, but I've never been abroad. But let's go anyway, somewhere far."

"We're not going for a picnic."

"You want to live somewhere far away, don't you? I can work and support us."

"You can?"

"Since I decided to come here with you, I've been thinking of marrying you. It's true."

"You're still in school."

"I've finished college. I'm in graduate school because I don't want to work. I'll quit school if you marry me."

It was hard to believe he was in graduate school, but I didn't think he would lie. Just as I'd been eager to have sex with him, I now felt a certain excitement in cornering him.

"You are still a dependent, so you have no idea how much money one needs to live on, even for a month. I detest living in poverty," I said.

"A dependent?"

I held Shunsuke's hand under the table while I kept my eyes on a young waiter in a white jacket and black tie. The way he was standing indicated he was a temporary. He didn't deal with the diners like the other waiters did. As I continued staring at him, his white jacket and trousers disappeared, and he became a naked man, looking down at his feet. I wanted to say something to him. I was already imagining having sex with him.

Shunsuke's gloom, which until now had been hidden deep inside him, started to surface. Just a short while ago his body had been on top of mine. He had looked like a gymnast on the horse, his legs and arms stretching and bending; in the end he had collapsed with a low cry. Now he was in front of me, dressed in his clothes, eating and talking about work. The time Shunsuke spent naked in bed with this woman was now forever sealed; it floated in the air, untouched, while real time passed. No one else could see how Shunsuke had changed in this passage of time. A male peacock spreads his feathers to show off before a female prior to copulation; the human male gives gifts to a woman whom he is going to marry. Someone once told me these are parallel courtship rituals. It is only humans who attempt to seal away what has come out of their sexual intercourse. The semen that came out of Shunsuke, so boyish and not very sexual, was left floating in the toilet bowl; it got there after passing through a woman's body. Shunsuke entered a woman's body without spreading his feathers. Now he had removed himself from all smell of sex and had talked about supporting this woman. I enjoyed this contradiction. In Shunsuke, whose outward appearance was asexual, I had nonetheless detected, like an animal with a keen nose, the smells of maleness and sex—and these smells compelled me to seduce him.

"You don't have to worry," he was saying. It was as if his voice came from a far distance. I was imagining that I was an animal quietly eating the food brought to me in my cave by a young man called Shunsuke. At that moment I had a feeling which people might call happiness, a sensation I hadn't experienced before. It hovered in the air momentarily, then disappeared.

"In this faraway place what would I do all day while you work?" I asked. I intended to let myself fall into the chasm of happiness, dragging Shunsuke along. I wanted to indulge myself for a while.

"You've lived forty years already. You can take it easy, sleep."

"I'll probably date another young man."

"You won't make me give up. I'm going to marry you. I don't give up easily once I make up my mind."

We bantered like this for a while before returning home. My anger had increased so much by then that I was ready to kick Shunsuke and be rid of him.

The relationship established through sex with Shunsuke made it clear to me that I could hope to live as an animal. I believed that the happiness I would gain then would surpass even the rapture of sexual climax, when we momentarily forget everything else. Men who boast of their skill in giving women sexual pleasure have never interested me because of this belief. To live as an animal would mean to give up both physical relationships and words. For this reason Shunsuke's sexuality would have to be destroyed, just as straw dogs are burned after the festivities.

I dialed the number printed on the matchbook I'd picked up at the hotel. I wanted to speak with that tall, temporary waiter. I had managed to obtain his name from another waiter. "That tall waiter is Mr. Yamamoto, isn't he," I asked. I got the response I wanted: "No. That's Unno." As I dialed, I remembered my excitement at hearing his name.

Rin'ichi Unno probably came out of curiosity.

"You remember me having a dinner with a young man, don't you?" I said to him.

"People often approach me like that," he responded.

"You're approached by customers often, then?"

"I'd say so. But I usually say no. If the manager finds out, he'll fire me," said Rin'ichi.

"Even temporary employees?"

"I'm not a temporary. I have another month of provisional status, though. I dropped out of high school so that's why I have to work hard."

"Well, I appreciate that you've come then. I wanted to see you, you know."

"What do you want by seeing me?"

"I want to go to bed with you."

"You say things very bluntly," said Rin'ichi, averting his eyes from me and looking down.

Rin'ichi glanced at his wrist watch, then he lit a cigarette. His fingers were unusually long. I imagined that those fingers were going to touch my body. He ground out his half-smoked cigarette in the ashtray, took out another and tapped it on the table. I watched the movements of his bony, slender fingers. He wore a blue jacket, and perhaps because of it, his face looked a bit pale.

"When I approach a girl, I don't say things as directly as you do," he said, forcing a smile.

"Do you do it as they do in the old-fashioned love stories then?"

"Girls like that, you know."

I felt my desire to have sex (which is not the same as sexual desire) quickly fading as I listened to this young man sitting across the table.

"Why did you pick me?" he asked as he stretched his long legs under the table.

Why did I pick this man: a waiter who looked like a kid working as a temporary? He wore exactly the same uniform as the rest of the waiters. My eyes had spotted him among several other men who looked the same. Why indeed had my eyes settled on this particular man, Rin'ichi Unno? But they had, and that seemed enough. Yet Rin'ichi asked me to explain. Does he want me to say that he looked particularly handsome among all those in uniform, or that he made a good impression on me? Does he want us to go through those same lines: "Why do you like me?" "Because I do."

That my eyes went to Eikichi, Yōji, Shunsuke and then

Rin'ichi, seemed to be the same as when some people are always noticing strange-looking plants with large flowers, while others are absorbed by looking at dilapidated houses, or the faces of old people. It wasn't that my eyes simply fell on these young men. Rather I'd say that they had seemed larger than life to me, as if I were looking at them through a magnifying glass. Eikichi came along when I'd told him I'd treat him to a steak; he hadn't asked why. When he'd finished eating his steak, he took off his clothes as if he were about to take a bath. I didn't have to say that I wanted to go to bed with him.

"I think women shouldn't say those things so openly," said Rin'ichi. "Of course women have sexual desire, too," he added.

"Sexual desire?" I said in a low voice, which came out of me in spite of myself, like vomit.

"Yes. I said women have sexual desire."

"That's obvious. But I don't, you can bet on it."

"But you said you wanted to go to bed with me."

"Wanting to go to bed and feeling sexual desire are two different things."

"How old are you really? Young women don't say things like that. Men have pride, if you really want to know," said Rin'ichi, smiling at me.

"I feel a lot of sexual desire now, but I don't feel like going to bed with you." I smiled as I stood up.

Outside, the street was full of people sightseeing. There were small children everywhere. Because it's a holiday, I thought. I walked, trying to avoid them, thinking they looked like worms emerging from their holes all at once. When I'd had dinner with Shunsuke, I had spotted Rin'ichi standing several feet away, rather than the other waiter who was in charge of our table. But why? Rin'ichi had been holding a silver tray, yet he looked to me as if he were standing there naked. Come to think of it, Yōji Tomoda, too, was there—a glass of beer in his hand, naked. It was the same with Eikichi and Shunsuke.

Children were running around, raising dust from the pavement. I saw a roller coaster silhouetted against the distant sky. It must have been moving slowly but from where I stood it looked like it was standing still. I walked, drinking 7-Up from a bottle. How did I appear in men's eyes, I wondered. I didn't have a "look" to label me with a certain job, to show I was a wife, or a mother. The sky was pale blue and flat as a photograph. I went toward the amusement park, looking for a man I wanted to have sex with. If I found one, I wanted to do it on the spot. If I caught a man looking at me, wouldn't that mean that he wanted to have sex with me, too? Rin'ichi must have come with such an intention, but my interest in having sex with him had left me before we began a physical relationship. My humiliation passed through him without touching him.

I sat on a bench by a large pond near the center of the amusement park. A drake was gliding on the water in front of me, and a child was throwing bread. There was, as always, a parent nearby, and when the child uttered a word or two, the parent responded. The drake was leaving silently. If mankind did not reproduce we'd get to the end rather quickly, and that would be good, I thought. But the moment I entertained this thought, a shiver of fear came over me; I thought people might see through me. I crouched on the bench, trying to shut out the inquiring eyes of passersby.

I saw an oden shop, which was covered in front with a reed screen.

"What time do you close?" I asked a young man, seventeen or eighteen perhaps, who brought me a beer. He gazed at me intently for a moment and said that the shop closed at five. His eyes smiled faintly. Déja vù, I thought: I've witnessed this scene before; I've been a part of a scene just like this. Although he was tall, the waiter could have been as young as fourteen or fifteen. And yet his male splendor was shining in his eyes as he looked at me.

"We close at five, isn't that right?" he asked someone as he went to the back of the shop. He sounded guileless. "A customer's asking," he said as he disappeared into the back room. Then I heard a low male laugh seeping out of that room.

I'm going to sit down on the bench outside and wait until five, I thought. He'll come out of that room sooner or later. He can't die in there.

I am repeating the same behavior, I said to myself, as I stood in the warm wind which swirled dust around me. I had patiently waited for Izumi Motofuji in a dry, cold wind. I would wait exactly as I had before and then I would make love to this young man who would soon come out of that shop. There were some taxis waiting outside the amusement park entrance. I would lead the young man into one of those taxis, like a kidnapper, and take him somewhere. Between the shop and the taxis was only about a hundred feet. I could get him to the car without difficulty. I would say something that would interest him. While I walked with him, I would take his hand or hold his arm, acting like it was natural for me to do so. The shorter the process of getting to sex, the better.

Rin'ichi had wanted to enjoy not the intercourse itself, but the ritual surrounding it, an affair. Izumi Motofuji, age seventeen, had taken a taxi with me to my house; he'd left immediately after having sex. And he had gone forever. His face had been blank. He had twisted his lips stubbornly as if saying he would never confess under torture. He won't ever tell, I thought, remembering his expression. I believed he wouldn't give in easily. A gentle accomplice to a small crime, that's what he'd been. He hadn't asked why I was interested in him. He came to my house with his school bag on his shoulder. When he took off his black school uniform, a plastic box full of English vocabulary cards fell from the pocket. He hadn't even asked my name. The intercourse had ended very quickly, but I had felt a physical connection with him. Izumi's sex organ had entered my body. Excited, it functioned as if it had a separate life. Izumi hadn't seemed to be aware of the possibility that his penis was there to excite the woman and give her pleasure, that he could pierce the woman and her pleasure together like a skewer for barbecuing chicken and onions.

What withers away after repeated sex that goes on and on like the rainy season is enthusiasm, but that isn't all; the relationship itself dies. Pleasure seekers often refuse to acknowlege the point at which the height of pleasure reaches a plateau. With their bodies, they risk the extinction of their sense of self, and yet their bodies also assist this same self as it tries to crawl out of its extinction. When one holds tightly to a sense of self during sexual pleasure, one's partner becomes a mere physical object. Such relationships soon give way to disillusionment. Two people who lie side by side after orgasm are merely two bodies, breathing hard, emptied out, powerless and incapable of anything, like large rotted fish washed up on a shore. Those who go after pleasure are forcing out their bodily fluid. I'm not that type of pleasure seeker.

People were leaving the amusement park. The shop was

still open, and I could see the young man moving around in the shop. He seemed to be cleaning up before closing. He wore a short white apron, like a chef's apron. Would he come out at five o'clock? Would he say the same things as Rin'ichi had? Or, would he, like Izumi Motofuji, come with me shamelessly?

A man who looked twenty-seven or twenty-eight sat on the bench across from me. He was smoking a cigarette and staring at the pond. He wore pale trousers and a thin, light-green jacket, suitable attire for a holiday outing. A lone woman was a rare sight in this recreation park, where most of the visitors were with families, and occasionally in pairs. It was also unusual to see a man alone. The man in the light-green jacket appeared to be an ordinary white-collar worker. He looked tired and seemed to be resting on the bench. He was smoking a cigarette. I was attracted to his ordinariness.

"Does the park close at five, do you know?" I asked when he looked toward me.

"Since it's a holiday today I think they close at six. That thing over there is still moving," he said, pointing at the ferris wheel.

"I see. But I don't think they'll let me on now."

"I think they will. I bet they'll operate it for even one passenger."

The large reed screen in front of the shop had been removed now, and a middle-aged man was closing the glass doors at the back. I couldn't see the young man in the white apron. But he should have been coming out any moment. He had no idea that he'd attracted a woman, and the other men in the shop probably didn't think he was particularly attractive to women. Even among children, some will stand out as sexual beings in the eyes of adults of the opposite sex. Women who look quite ordinary in other women's eyes are sometimes attractive to men. It's the same with men. This mystery will never be solved.

"It's five already, isn't it?" I asked the man in the light-green jacket.

"What? Oh yes," he said, looking at his watch.

"Why don't we ride on that thing over there?" I said, keeping my eyes on the shop.

"What?" He turned his head to look at me.

"Do you want to ride it and then go somewhere?" I said again.

"That wheel?" He stood up.

"Yes, ride it and then go somewhere far. . . ."

The man was about to leave, ignoring me, but he came back and stared at me.

"I think we'll be able to see everything from there, all the people. And then, we can go somewhere far from here and. . . ." I trailed off, looking up the man. He looked away as if trying to avoid a light glaring in his eyes. Then he looked at the ground like a child who didn't know what to say.

At that moment I saw a boy, four or five years old, running toward us.

"Why don't we go somewhere?" I repeated.

"What do you mean by that? What are you doing here anyway?"

"Daddy!" the child was nearing us, still running.

"What I mean is that we should go somewhere and have a good time."

"You're crazy, aren't you? This is where kids have fun." The man raised his voice and several people walking with their children stopped. The man raised his voice even more. "You're insane, trying to pick up a man at a place like this. Something's wrong with you."

Now people were staring at us and beginning to crowd around us.

"Daddy," the child called and ran to the man, who, still talking loudly, picked up his son. Then he put the child down and hid him behind his back, as if to protect him from me.

"This is a place for children to have fun," he repeated. "So don't you say anything weird. I'll call the police if necessary."

The man was standing with his feet slightly apart, shielding his son. He looked like a mother protecting her child against an enemy. The number of spectators was increasing.

"Let's go, Daddy, Mom wants you to come," said the child, pulling the man's hand.

I sat there stiffly, both hands gripping the bench. I might have looked like a person with a terrible stomachache. From an opening in the wall of people that surrounded me I stealthily watched the oden shop. Parents and children stared at me; I heard voices from behind the wall of people, asking what was happening. The young father left, holding his son's hand and repeating words of reassurance: "It's all right." Other people began moving on.

Absent-mindedly, I tried to remember what I'd said to the man. He'd taken my words "have a good time" as an attempt to lure him into a sexual encounter. I felt like a person who, after realizing he has been a victim of extortion, still can't help being impressed by the skill with which the scheme was pulled off. When I said "have a good time," I meant having sex. But I didn't mean to "allure" him. And what did he mean by saying to his child, "It's all right"?

The oden shop was closed now, but no one came out. At the back of the shop was a high stone wall, so even if the young man had left from the rear he would still have to come around to the front where I was watching. I couldn't have missed him. A middle-aged man had gone toward the back door earlier; he must have gone inside. I'd seen a few men going into the shop, but none had come out. I heard a loudspeaker announcing that the park was closing at six. I saw someone pulling a brown curtain across the glass door of the shop. Several long tables and small plastic chairs that had been outside were all gone now. Without those tables and chairs and the reed screen, the shop looked naked. Someone had been cooking oden in back, but no one had come out yet. It was a small, shabby establishment with reed screens on three sides.

There have to be several men in that shop, I kept thinking. That young man who looked seventeen or eighteen and another fellow were waiters, and it seemed there were two or three more in the back room of the shop. Another man went in. He wore a grey shirt, like those worn by the men who worked in the flower garden. Now many people were walking toward the gate but I sat on the bench in front of the oden shop, watching. There was less than five feet between me and the shop. I couldn't have missed. . . .

Two more men in grey shirts went into the shop, this time through the front glass door. A grey shirt seemed to be the uniform of the park employees.

A man in a grey shirt came up to me and told me that the park was closing. There was no one around except me. I stood up pretended to walk toward the gate, but when the man had gone, I sat on the bench again. The man who'd told me the park was closing also went inside the shop. Then, a few minutes afterward, another four or five men went in; they paid no attention to me. Yet no one had come out of the shop. The back of the shop was a high wall of rocks over which tree branches hung heavily.

Even while the man with the child was loudly protesting my conduct, I'd kept a watch on the shop through the cracks in the wall of spectators. I hadn't seen that young man come out of the shop. I was no longer thinking of him, however. Instead, I gazed at the shop, the cheaply assembled building. As I watched the building intently, it seemed to swell. Since more men had gone inside, it had expanded. Now, two more went toward the back door. It was getting dark, the twilight setting like mist. Two men in grey shirts came toward me, pulling a large metal trash can. There was no doubt now that the shirt was a workmen's uniform. They saw me but didn't tell me to leave.

How many had gone into the shop? I'd lost count. Although it was now dark, there was no light inside. But I kept watching the shop from the bench by the pond. I had lost interest in the young man—my interest was now focused on the small shop where they sold oden. The small, cottage-like building had swelled up with so many men inside. I was not interested in those men. I simply found it amazing that so many men could fit inside. Another group of men went in but now it was impossible to tell whether they wore grey uniforms. There were at least ten. Then, another black shadow appeared from the direction of the big wheel and disappeared into the shop. I wondered if there might be a tunnel connecting the back door to somewhere outside. Otherwise it was a complete mystery. Lights went on here and there in the park, and a lamp near the bench where I sat formed a circle of bright light around me.

People could see me well now. The shop just stood there, still dark inside. In the darkness outside, it was swelling. From that building they should be able to see me well. But no one was coming out to tell me to leave.

The Marsh

Yūko Tsushima

"It's called the Round Marsh because it's round. That's all there is to its name," he told me.

His explanation made me think of a marsh I remember called the Small Marsh. This marsh was on top of a hill, right next to a larger marsh, which was naturally called the Big Marsh. I saw these two marshes years ago when I was in middle school. It was summer, and I was spending a few days near the marshes with my friend and her family.

Although I recall their names, I've forgotten what the Big Marsh looked like. I do remember the Small Marsh, though I haven't had any reason to think about it until now, when I suddenly find myself fascinated by the memory of it as if I had never forgotten about it, not even for a day.

The Small Marsh was also round. It had dark, still water at the bottom of its cone-shaped landform and its rim was slightly elevated. It was small enough for children to walk around easily; in fact it looked like a big puddle. I learned that the water from the nearby Big Marsh seeped underground and welled up to form the Small Marsh. Before this was discovered, people were mystified by the source of its water. Having grown up in the city, I couldn't understand what was so mysterious about water appearing in the middle of a mountain. At the time I listened to the explanations absent-mindedly, but now I realize what an impression the marsh made on me.

My friend's family told me that we were heading for the Small Marsh, but when I actually saw it from high up on the mountain path, I felt something that I couldn't explain. Even now I clearly remember the feeling that I had seen something I shouldn't have, something monstrous.

It was very quiet around the marsh and the scene was desolate. There were no trees or plants nearby, only black mud and turbid water. The stillness of the water reminded me of mercury. For a moment I was overcome by the belief that the marsh had the power to suck things in and swallow them whole. I wanted to run in the other direction.

Of course my fear was only momentary, and soon I was racing down the path toward the marsh with my friend. We ran all around it. It was in fact a popular sightseeing spot and there were a lot of people there that day. It wasn't a place where one should feel scared. The water was calm with occasional ripples breaking its surface. Still, because the bank was wet, there was some danger of slipping into the mud. Perhaps this was the main reason there were no restaurants, not even benches for people to sit on, although it was a part of the sightseeing route. We didn't stay there very long. The marsh was too small to make me feel nervous for long, and I quickly grew accustomed to its sight.

Probably because of the unknown origin of its water, there was a legend about the Small Marsh's guardian spirit. After all, it wasn't the kind of place where one wants to swim, and it didn't appear as though any fish or shellfish lived there. It didn't seem strange, therefore, that people imagined some mysterious creature living at the bottom of this barren-looking marsh. Certainly there might be one or two creatures which would grow to look like monsters after living in such a place.

The legend I was told at the time was quite an ordinary one. It went like this: The guardian spirit of the marsh fell in love with a man, and in order to live with him it changed its appearance to that of a woman. After the marsh spirit gave birth to a child, her true identity was revealed to her husband, and she was forced to return to the marsh, leaving her child behind. I thought at the time that it was an ordinary, uninteresting story, not unique to this marsh. I was more fascinated by the possibility that some grotesque creature might live at the bottom of the water.

The Small Marsh that I recall now, however, cannot be separated in my mind from the legend. I cannot think of it without hearing the suppressed breathing of a creature who longs for a human male.

I can see another marsh from the northern window of my apartment building. Since quite a few carp swim in the water and a few large stepping stones are arranged for a decorative effect, one should perhaps call this a pond, but I suspect it used to look more like a marsh before someone built it up. The pond is long and skinny, formed by the accumulation of water in the V-shaped crack at the bottom of a cliff. It is hard to tell where the water comes from, but it is probably the same source that feeds the other similar marshes in the neighborhood—those in the park which was formerly someone's estate, in the shrine's compound, and on the University campus. These marshes lie at the bottom of some cliffs which divide the hills and the lowlands.

One part of the marsh I see from my apartment is in the garden of a mansion where many generations of a family have been living. The marsh's center is in front of a newly built high-rise condominium; the rest stretches out like a tail along the land where a company dormitory stands. The cliff is at the south end of the marsh, blocking the sun. The water doesn't seem to be deep since even a small amount of rain makes it muddy. I can see from my window only the tail-like part by the dormitory. Plastic bags, styrofoam cups and other pieces of trash float on the surface of the water. Still, there are a few carp and crayfish in the water, and I often see the custodian shouting at the neighborhood boys as they try to sneak onto the grounds to catch them.

My building is in a neighborhood where small houses and apartments line the narrow, winding streets. But if I lean my head out while sitting on the sill of the north window of my room on the second floor, I can see the marsh. Every time I see the water of the marsh shining with dull light, I find it surprising. Walking along the streets, one would never suspect a marsh is hidden nearby. The high-rise condominium and the large estate face the sunny side of the hill, which gives no hint of water. When I walk by this hill to go to the train station and the neighborhood grocery stores, it's hard to picture the marsh on the other side.

Perhaps it is because of the marsh that I feel uneasy in my room. I can't get rid of the feeling that the building might sink into the water. My children are also afraid of the marsh. When my six-year-old daughter refuses to listen to me, I sometimes open the north window and call, "Mr. Kappa[1] over there, do you want a little girl?" She becomes frightened and cries, hiding be-

---

[1] *A toad-like, imaginary creature which often appears in Japanese folk tales.*

hind my back. My two-year-old gets scared, too, and he retreats to the corner of the room crying, "I don't like kappas." Often an ominous feeling comes over me. Not just my children but I, too, cannot look down at the marsh for long.

And yet it was because of the marsh that I rented this apartment. I was surprised at my decision. I had just found out that I was pregnant with my second child. I knew that my lover's wife, also pregnant at the time with her second child, knew nothing of her husband's affair with me. I was upset with myself for wanting to keep the child, for trying to keep the child's father from leaving me by getting pregnant. I decided to move away without telling him. As long as I stayed where I was he would continue to come and see me, unable to resist his own desire, and I, for my part, would dream of having his babies as soon as he held me in his arms again. I wanted to live with him, to be in the same place and breathe the same air. But the more I became used to his body, the more he became a stranger to me. I was divorced and raising my daughter. I thought that if he, who had a life with his wife and child elsewhere, was a normal human being then I, whose existence was unknown, unseen and unacceptable to his family, had to be a creature without human form, like an evil spirit that inhabits the mountains and rivers. The thought that the man I loved didn't belong to the world I lived in filled me with despair. I couldn't resist thinking that if I bore his child, I would become one of his kind.

In my mind's eye the man's pregnant wife was my own mother. Just after I was born my mother learned that there was another woman about to have a child by my father. Shortly after this discovery, my father died, leaving my mother no chance to understand her relationship with him. Nonetheless, my mother didn't forget anything. For thirty years she has been obsessed with that other woman, whom she believes is the evil spirit of the mountains and rivers. What could the child of this evil spirit and her husband be like, and how could she, the legitimate wife, have given birth to his child as if nothing had happened? My mother has been endlessly haunted by these questions.

As for myself, when I learned of my second pregnancy I pictured this scene: upon finding out about my pregnancy, my lover's wife throws herself in front of a moving train, or from the top of a tall building. I was filled with fear that this scene would come true.

I felt obsessed with this vision and began living my days as if in a dream. I was looking for a new apartment in my dream, and one day I was shown a room facing a narrow alley. It was a dark room with the neighbors' wall blocking the sun, but the rent was cheap. When I opened the window on the north side, I immediately wanted to live there. The marsh I saw from the window was the one I had once seen, at another time.

Four years ago, there was no condominium or company dormitory there, just a large, empty lot. Because it was surrounded by tall walls, one couldn't tell that behind them was a wide open space.

I had just become friends with a woman. It was shortly after my husband and I had separated, and she and I each had two-year-old daughters. The father of my friend's daughter never appeared, but I didn't ask what had happened to him. She had apparently stopped seeing him before her daughter was born; it wasn't clear if he even knew about his child. Perhaps to him my friend was like the evil spirit of mountains and rivers, but to me she was a valued ally who taught me that mourning the loss of my child's father was silly. She was six years younger than I was, only twenty-two.

My friend and I saw each other almost every day. Sometimes I went to stay with her; other times she came to my apartment to spend the night. On weekends we went out with our daughters and walked around town. Then one day we discovered the vacant lot where the marsh was. We were excited about our discovery and immediately began exploring the place. Although we were a bit scared at the vastness of the space and the thick tangle of grasses growing there, we were as thrilled as our daughters. We laughed as we saw hydrangeas in bloom and laughed again as we took turns climbing up a large garden rock. Since there were overgrown shrubs all around, we could explore only a small area of the place. But when we forced our way through some tall bushes and sorrel vines, we found a long, skinny marsh. Beyond the bushes we saw a cliff, and at the bottom of the cliff was a body of dark water. We saw something move in the water. Terrified, we fled, making sure we didn't make any noise. When we reached the other side of the concrete wall, we found ourselves on an ordinary street. We heaved big sighs of relief, escaping what we had just seen. We thought that the marsh must be quite old and that the creature must have lived there for a long time—so long that it now looked like a monster. How big could it be and what did it look like? We talked about it for a while.

Our excitement lasted for some time. We promised each other we'd go back, but then I became involved with the father of my second child and I had little chance to see my friend. Around that time she began feeling anxious about her sexuality, and started acting strangely. She became afraid of the evil spirt of the mountains and rivers, which she felt was stirred up inside her as various men came in and out of her life. She was put into the psychiatric ward of a hospital by people who were alarmed by her behavior. It was difficult to visit her but we frequently talked on the phone. When I decided to move to my present apartment, I called her first.

"It's true, I can see our marsh from the back window," I told her. "A condominium and some company's dormitory stands on the lot now, and it looks quite different. But the marsh is still there. They probably wanted to fill it in but they couldn't. That's my guess. No, it doesn't look as if anything strange lives there; carp are swimming about instead. Compared to the time we saw it, it looks quite ordinary. But don't you think it's exciting that I can see it from my window? I want you to come and see it as soon as you can get permission to go out. It's no fun looking at it by myself. Only you and I knew about it. Right?"

It wasn't for quite a while, however, that she was able to come to my apartment. Even when she had permission to go out, she was required to spend the night at her parents' house.

Although I had managed to move away without telling the father of my baby, I couldn't change my job, and so within a week he found me and came to see me at my new apartment. Once he forced his way back into my life, I had no choice but to dream I could keep him as my own. His second child by his wife was born and, six months later, I also had my second child. He came to see how I was getting on with this newborn, and when he saw that I was becoming increasingly clinging and half-mad, he left me for good.

My baby has grown steadily. It's been more than two years since I moved to this room. More than a few people stopped being my friends when I had my second child, but I have made some new friends. I was a spirit of the mountains and rivers when I gave birth to this child but the child turned out to be a normal human being.

About a year and a half ago my friend was released from the hospital and returned to her parents' house. She sold insurance for awhile and then took the exams to become a nutritionist and a hygienic technician. She failed both exams. A few months ago she found work as a "lunch lady," a temporary position cooking at a school cafeteria. She seemed better suited to this job than anybody had expected. Her life became normal, and she began visiting me on Saturdays. She would stay until evening and then she'd go back to her parents' for supper. She almost always came to visit without advance notice. Sometimes I was out, and her visit would be wasted; other times her unexpected arrival would upset my plans. I found this irritating, but whenever I saw her plump face, I found myself smiling at her.

"This job is great for me," she told me the other day while she was playing with my younger child.

"I'm surprised how much I like it. The other lunch ladies are all older than me, and they pamper me. I get there an hour earlier than the others. No, I don't do anything in particular, I just wait for the rest to come. A big change for me, don't you think? Since I only work till four, my son doesn't have to wait for me too long when he gets home from school. I have no complaints now. I sometimes wonder if I should have some, though. I feel so comfortable. I don't seem to have a desire to change anything. No one will ever be seriously interested in me anyway. I can't think of marriage at this point, you know. My mother arranged for me to see this guy the other day. He's almost fifty years old, with three kids. His wife's dead, he told me. He didn't want to marry me though. 'You're young and pretty, you must have plenty of offers,' he said. A compliment perhaps. The age doesn't matter to me, but I don't feel like having a relationship with a man now. I think about our days a lot, though. Nowadays, I guess I'm what people call an education mama. Don't you think it's funny? I make my son take piano and swimming lessons. I nag him to study, although I myself watch television a lot. It somehow feels good to shout at your kid, you know. But I attend P.T.A. meetings regularly. I put makeup on and dress nicely. It's really interesting, because those mothers are so serious; they're always putting on airs. Most of the time I keep quiet, but once in a while I just have to let my true self out and say something. There was a meeting the day before yesterday, and some woman started talking about how she didn't know what to say when her kid kept asking about babies, how they are born, and so on. Everybody talked about it for a while. One person said it's too early to give them any facts, and the others looked so uncomfortable. I felt like teasing them and so I spoke up without thinking. It's an important issue, and we ought to give them accurate information, I said. I should've stopped there. But they were nodding their heads, you know. So I went ahead and told them how I would open my legs to let my kid see what's between them. I let him see the hole and told him that he came out of it, I told them. It's the same hole where men stick their penises and pour in this thing that makes babies. It's the hole that blood comes out of when babies are not made. I said I told my son all these things. They looked at me with shocked faces. Don't you think it's strange? I got a bit scared afterward and felt depressed. I felt I had said something silly again. . . ."

When she talked like this, I enjoyed listening. Ever since I heard about the Round Marsh, I've been wanting to ask her something. I want to ask her about the spirit of the marsh who falls in love with a human male and changes her appearance to have his child. Why is it that the spirit's true identity must be revealed? I don't understand why she has to leave. Besides, why does she have to leave her child behind? You and I keep our children, I want to tell my friend.

It is no longer clear to me whether we are the evil spirits of the mountains and rivers, or if the spirits are our lovers. Whichever they are, the children who were born are growing up normally, unconcerned with the questions I keep asking.

I heard about the Round Marsh from a man who happened to find it while he was driving through the mountains. He told me he was surprised by his discovery. The marsh he spotted at a distance down from the road looked quite desolate and forbidding. He had never heard that there was a marsh in that area, and because it looked so quiet he felt a bit uneasy. There is an old inn by the marsh, he said. It was quite dark around the inn, even during the day, because it was deep in the forest. How would one feel staying overnight at such an inn? he asked me. He also told me that he found out the name of the marsh afterward.

Since then I have been thinking about the Round Marsh, which lies even deeper in the mountain than the Small Marsh.

Somewhere high up in the mountain is a road, shining in the sun. I see a small dot on the road, a white car driven by the man who told me about the Round Marsh. Perpendicular to the road is the mountain, which stretches all the way up from the road and down. The surface of the mountain is smooth, and it looks as if the slope is spiraling down into the marsh. The water of the marsh shines darkly. The surrounding virgin forest gives off a sound like the moaning of a person in pain, and by the water's edge is the creature of the marsh. From a distance it looks like a house, and it crouches, longing for a human male.

I want to go to see the Round Marsh. My longing is getting stronger every day, but I haven't been able to tell the man who described it to me that I want to visit it with him. I am merely gazing at this man, with whom I became acquainted on some unexpected occasion.

About the Editor and Translator

Yukiko Tanaka, Ph.D., was born in Yokohama, Japan. She came to live in the United States in 1969, where she earned her doctorate in comparative literature from the University of California, Los Angeles. She co-edited and co-translated *This Kind of Woman: Ten Stories by Japanese Women Writers, 1960–1976* (Stanford University Press, 1982). She has also edited and translated *To Live and To Write: Selections by Japanese Women Writers 1913–1938,* (Seal Press, 1987). She has recently completed a history of Japanese women writers from the beginning of the modern era through World War II, as well as a study of the lives and opinions of contemporary Japanese women. She has translated a number of stories for various journals and anthologies.

Welcome to the World of International Women's Writing

Two Women in One by Nawal el-Saadawi. $9.95. ISBN:1-879679-01-9

One of this Egyptian feminist's most important novels, *Two Women in One* is the story of Bahiah Shaheen, a well-behaved Cairo medical student, a girl who keeps out of trouble and obeys her father's orders. But it is also the story of the "other" Bahiah—rebellious, political, artistic, full of repressed desires.

How Many Miles to Babylon by Doris Gercke. $8.95. ISBN: 1-879679-02-7

Hamburg Police detective Bella Block needs a vacation. She thinks she'll find some rest in the countryside, but after only a few hours in the remote village of Roosbach, she realizes she has stumbled on to one of the most troubling cases of her career. An engrossing mystery featuring a tough new heroine, *How Many Miles to Babylon* is the first of wildly popular Doris Gercke's provocative thrillers to be translated into English.

Originally established in 1984 as an imprint of Seal Press, Women in Translation is now a nonprofit publishing company dedicated to making women's writing from around the world available in English translation. We specialize in anthologies, thrillers and literary fiction. The books above may be ordered from us at 3131 Western Ave, Suite 410, Seattle WA 98121 (please include $2.00 postage and handling for the first book and .50 for each additional book). Write to us for a free catalog.